Through Crystal Clear Waters

Susan D. Shevlane

Copyright© 2012 by Susan D. Shevlane
All rights reserved

ISBN: 1475010664
ISBN-13: 9781475010664

Library of Congress Control Number: 2012904538
CreateSpace, North Charleston, South Carolina

Author Biography

Susan D. Shevlane, born in 1953, has written poetry and short stories from an early age. Susan has been published in the International Library of Poetry, gained an Editor's Choice award, and was nominated for a poetry award in New York. Susan writes articles on a writers' website, https://www.helium.com on topics such as humanities, religion, and philosophy and has worked as a journalist at a community newspaper, *The Inner Nottingham Gazette.* Having had many articles published about local events, cultural diversities, politics, and stories about people from all walks of life, Susan is launching her first novel after being encouraged to do so from people familiar with her work.

Susan is the mother of six children and lives in the Midlands of England. She also spends time in Texas with her brother, using the tranquil setting to write.

I am sure we are going to see more work evolving from this talented author.

-Paul C. Hackett, musician/project specialist

Through Crystal Clear Waters

Introduction

A woman in her late fifties, Chiane, who has had precognitive dreams since abandoned at birth, embarks on a journey to the Caribbean. Having no ancestral roots of her own, she has spent a lifetime trying to discover who she really is, despite overcoming all the many obstacles life has thrown at her.

Guided by her dreamtime mentor/ spirit guide, 'Izacal', she lands for a one month stay in Jamaica. She had visited Jamaica before, but spent most of the time in the tourist area. This time was going to be different, as she was to spend the whole time up on a rural hilltop in Clarendon, deep in the country where water had to be fetched from a standpipe halfway down the hill and the general living was very basic.

On the second day there, she meets up with the great-great grandson of Izacal, who takes her on mystical journeys to discover past, present and future revelations of mankind. She learns about the fate of Atlantis, the predictions of the Mayan and North American Indians and discovers the ancient power of crystals. By the time she returns home to England, she soon finds events are about to mystically change her life.

What happens next takes her on more adventures attempting to seek the truth, to different locations, accompanied by an old friend, Dusty, a well known archeologist.

Beginning in Mexico, finding a Mayan artifact that holds the secret of the 5th and 6th Mayan calendars, and the truth about December 21st 2012. They are kidnapped by a drugs cartel, escape and return to the States. The next adventure is to find where to take this precious artifact, which leads the two friends on a journey with the Cherokee across the Indian Territories of North America, to find the people prophesied to obtain the object. They learn of the events due to take place from December 2012 into the future cycle calendars, the warnings, teachings and prophesy of the ancients, with a conclusion that opens the door to the next cycle of humanity. Chiane also finds out exactly who she is, and discovers what she must do to fulfill her future life path!

Along with the sights and sounds of rural Jamaica, Mexico & Native America, this fictional story blurs the edges of fact and fiction, taking the reader on a soul searching, adventurous, educational journey.

Dedications and Acknowledgements

To the memory of Hugh Anthony Joseph Shevlane.

Many thanks to my family for their support, to my friend Robin for encouraging me to follow my dreams and ambitions, and to my brother, Paul, for making it all possible and giving me advice.

Contents

Chapter 1	Beginnings	1
Chapter 2	The Dream	9
Chapter 3	The Journey	15
Chapter 4	Island Life	25
Chapter 5	The Meeting	37
Chapter 6	The Gift	49
Chapter 7	The Ancients	55
Chapter 8	The Crystal	61
Chapter 9	Mankind Drowning	69
Chapter 10	Summing Up	77
Chapter 11	Going Home	89
Chapter 12	Reality	95
Chapter 13	Taking a chance	107
Chapter 14	Into the unknown	115
Chapter 15	The Secret	125
Chapter 16	Destiny	131
Chapter 17	Kidnapped	143
Chapter 18	Dusty's Secret	157
Chapter 19	Izacal returns	167
Chapter 20	Izacal's Instructions	177
Chapter 21	The Test	183
Chapter 22	Journey with the Cherokee	195
Chapter 23	Enlightenment	205
Chapter 24	Into the Future	219
Chapter 25	The Star Children	237

Chapter 1

Beginnings

The last few months had seen me troubled with dreams. It felt as though when I was sleeping, someone was trying to tell me "you know what you must do!"

Dreams had been important to me as a child; visions, too, had been a regular occurrence for as long as I could remember. I knew nothing of my background, as I was left in the hospital in Leicestershire, England, as a baby. No surname; no details of my parents; just a birth certificate that named me Chiane.

June 1, 1953, the day before the coronation of Queen Elizabeth, I entered this world. I was actually presented with a silver spoon from the government to mark the occasion, so I suppose you could say I was born with a silver spoon in my mouth. That should mean a rosy life ahead, according to the quotation, but in reality things never quite go according to plan. I had blonde hair, but I also had olive skin and dark-brown eyes, which in those days was not so

Through Crystal Clear Waters

advantageous. The local authority seemed to have a problem with my skin tone. Because of my "mixed blood," I was not allowed to go to the local adoption agency—I was not thought good enough for decent people to adopt. So along with two other babies, who were the products of black American servicemen, I remained under the care of the sister in charge until I could be "back-door" adopted. At three months old, I went to live on a farm in rural Lincolnshire where I was fostered by a couple in their forties, and the following year they adopted me.

The people in the neighbouring village would always say to my adoptive mother: "It's a dangerous thing to adopt. You don't know who the father is," or "Look at her colour; she does not fit in!" But the most popular one of all was, "She is not like us; she is different."

Even when I started school, they didn't give up. By this time my hair had turned dark brown and my skin colour was still as tanned, so I still looked foreign, especially with my dark-brown eyes. I loved to read and learn, but teachers, classmates and the people in the village commented, "Do you think you're better than us?" and again, "You are different."

This didn't bother me. In fact, it gave me strength. They wanted to bring me down, put me in my place, but I liked being different. I did not want to be like them.

My mother always told me that they had chosen me when they adopted me, and I should never forget that I was a "chosen one" when people tried to put me down. They only said hurtful things because they were not chosen. They were ordinary.

Because I was special, I thought I had carte blanche to do what I wanted and get away with it. I would scrump up a tree and throw apples down to the other kids, but I never got caught when the farmer came to march them to their parents. I had a vantage point high up in the tree and knew when to keep still and quiet.

When some monks came to the village to write their manuscripts, my parents and teachers were looking all over to find me. The old man that cut the hedgerows said, "You can bet you will find her with them monks," and sure enough, there I was, helping them and listening to their teachings. I didn't get into trouble, though. I mean, what could they say? I just smiled and told them I was learning about Jesus. Oh yes, I was certainly different.

I had my friends in the dream world, who would help guide me through life and tell me of things that were to happen. Things would happen just as they did in my dreams. Usually they were silly things. I would

Through Crystal Clear Waters

dream of someone visiting, and the next day, that same person would turn up on the doorstep, or a turn of events happened just as I had dreamt them a few nights before.

Sometimes, when I told my mother of the dreams and how they came true, she became frightened and got angry, telling me not to talk of such things. She told me that people would not understand and would give me a hard time.

And so I grew up, got married, and left the village. I always had my dreams and visions but would only tell those I was close to about them. When I became pregnant for the fourth time, I was plagued with a Latin phrase, *Kyrie eleison*, which kept going round and round in my head, rather like a song you have just heard on the radio and cannot forget. My husband, Hugh, who knew Latin, told me the meaning translated as "Lord have mercy." I told him I had this feeling that something was going to happen to either me or the pope. Most people would have laughed at such a statement, but Hugh knew not to take my eccentricities for granted. He had many a time been witness to things I told him would happen, but this latest one worried him and he became concerned for my well-being.

In February of 1981, when I was about four-and-a-half months pregnant, I lost the baby, and almost lost my own life, too. Only a blood transfusion saved me.

Beginnings

During that time, I was "clinically dead." I felt I was above looking down on myself, watching the doctors, hearing what they were saying, until they injected me with something and I felt myself returning to my body. The doctors were amazed at what I told them. They said, "It is impossible. You were out for the count." Three months later, on May 13, the pope was shot in the stomach. He, too, was in a hospital fighting for his life.

After I recovered, I didn't have literal dreams anymore but dreamt in parables. This meant I had to work the dreams out, which was sometimes difficult to do. At times the dreams' meanings only became apparent after something had happened, and I could only look back in reflection. But that was how it was.

I had three more children and thought that was what my life was all about: being married, bringing up the children, keeping house, and going to work. My world didn't seem to have time to work out dreams, or pay attention to feelings and visions. But I always felt that something was missing, that there was something I must do. From childhood, I had written stories, poems, and songs, but lately I had not even had time to write.

I began to feel as if I had forgotten who I was and what I had wanted from life. My mind reflected back onto the first song I had written when I was eight years old. I knew I must get back in touch with who I was. I wrote the words down again and read them out loud to myself.

Listen to the thunder

Look at the lightening

Have you ever stopped to wonder?

Why is it so frightening?

Here it comes again now

Does it hurt your eye?

Have you ever stopped to think how?

Where, when, or why

People walking aimlessly

About the street

Never stop to think about

The folk they're gonna meet

They just carry on regardlessly

But that sort of life

Beginnings

Isn't good enough for me

As I remembered myself as a child, waiting to take the world on, I wondered where all that spirit had gone. I loved my husband and children, but something was missing. I needed to do what I liked doing best. My ambitions to travel were grounded, or at least put on hold till the children grew up. But I decided to get back in tune with myself and start writing again, and to study all the things I used to be interested in before I joined the rat race. So between my shifts at the factory, looking after the children, and keeping house, I took myself off down to the library every spare moment I had, studying world cultures, astrology, astronomy, and philosophy.

That seemed to satisfy me, for a while at least. But one day in 1992, my husband died. My whole world turned upside down, and I relocated with my four youngest children to Nottingham, to try and make a fresh start for myself and my family. It was hard going, but I still found time to study and enrol in college, as well as work and bring up the children. I was so exhausted that even if I did dream, I did not remember. I was too busy getting on with life.

Chapter 2

The Dream

Ten years had now passed since the death of my husband and our move to the city, and the dreams were beginning again. There seemed to be an urgency about them, and it was making me anxious. It began with a message from an old Rasta man sitting up in a tree, which I stood under. He told me a poem that I quickly wrote down on waking, lest I should forget it.

Indian man sits on a mountain high

Gives his praises to the sky

While horses run and eagles fly

Indian believes he will never die

Black man high up in a big tall tree

Looking out on all he can see

Through Crystal Clear Waters

Singing songs of how he should be free
From the beginning of time till eternity

White man sits on a prickly pine
Says this goddamned world is mine, all mine
He's trampled the grapes from the holy vine
Thinks he will hold power till the end of time

After that, a bird visited my dreams. As I walked through a land rich in vegetation, sparkling rivers, and clear blue sky, the small white bird would fly in front of me, as if showing me where to walk. I would follow. This happened for about six nights. On the seventh night, the little bird led me to a large expanse of water; I looked upon the huge lake and watched the sun glistening on the ripples just like stars in the night. I sat down on a rock underneath a tree at the edge of the lake, where the little bird had perched on one of the branches. All of a sudden, whilst I was taking in the beautiful scenery, the bird flew off across the lake. I felt sad because I knew that this time I could not follow. I woke up, thought about the dream, and wondered if I would ever see the little white bird again.

The Dream

For the next few weeks I still visited the lake in my dreams and tried to find my way around it. Without the little bird to guide me, I met with all sorts of obstacles, but each night I managed to get a bit further. Sometimes in the morning I would wake feeling exhausted by the travels in my sleep.

Then one night, about four weeks after the little bird had disappeared, I reached a bridge over a narrow part of the lake. It was a single footbridge made of neatly tied bamboo and rope stretching from one rocky side of the lake to the other, dipping in the middle. There, perched on the rope handrail, was the little bird, his head cocked to one side, watching me as I approached the footbridge. As soon as I reached the bridge, the little bird started to fly across, and without hesitation, I followed. We soon reached the other side of the lake, and the little bird flew up into the rocks where there was a large cave. Sitting at the mouth of the cave was a young man of about eighteen or nineteen; I climbed the rocks up to the cave and sat down in front of him.

He was a handsome young fellow with athletic stature and a rich bronzed tan. He had long, jet-black hair, neatly tied back, and he gazed at me with the darkest brown eyes I had ever seen. He was clad in a pure white toga tied at the waist with a rope that seemed to be made out of pure gold, and wore sandals on his feet.

Through Crystal Clear Waters

The young man told me his name was Izacal and that he had been waiting a long time for me to come. As he spoke, he seemed to breathe an air of calm and I immediately felt at peace.

"You are to make a journey," he said, "far away from your life now. You are to leave your fast Western life behind and reach a place where you will find what you believe you lost many years ago." He told me he would be with me, although I may not see him, and that he would guide me, showing me what I needed to know. Then the young man got up. "Rest now, for soon your journey will begin." He disappeared into the cave. I lay down to rest and the next thing I knew, I was waking up to another day.

As I reflected on the dream, I remembered one Bonfire Night when I was a child, when I had looked up at the stars and saw what looked like a Greek god, travelling across the sky on a chariot without any horse. I had pointed the vision out to my mother, who said, "Yes, dear," but told me the next morning she had not seen anything. Was the young man in my dream the same young man I had seen all those years ago?

I thought about what he had said and realised that in about two months, I was due to fly to Jamaica to spend four weeks with my friend Eli, who had invited

The Dream

me to visit him and his family, deep in the countryside there. Although I had visited Jamaica with Eli before, this time it was to be different. That first time had been mostly spent in the tourist area. This time, I was to go deep into the heart of Jamaica, high on a mountain, where the people lived a simple, basic life. There would be no indoor toilets, and water was either caught in a barrel when it rained or brought uphill in containers from a standpipe on the main road. There, I would be definitely leaving my Western life behind. Was this the journey the young man in my dream was talking about?

As I got ready to go to work that morning, I wondered if I would find what it was I believed I had lost many years ago, and if I would see Izacal again. Somehow this day seemed to have a different meaning than all the others. I was beginning to think that things would never be the same again.

Chapter 3

The Journey

Two months soon passed. I found myself checking everything needed for my flight the next day. Since that last dream when I had met Izacal, I had not had any more dreams and had got on with my day-to-day living.

My children were staying the night, prior to my departure. My youngest daughter Kathleen, now known as Katie, was quite excited at having the house to herself for the next month, and my next daughter Maria was about to move into her own house with her baby son Darnell. We had spent the last two months decorating and preparing the house, which she was due to move into a couple of weeks after I left, along with her elder sister Bridget, and brother James, who were helping with the move. We sat together with a Chinese take-away and a bottle of wine, chatting the evening away until it was time to retire.

I woke around 4:00 a.m. and prepared for my long journey. A taxi was to pick me up at 5:30 a.m. for the

Through Crystal Clear Waters

three-hour trip from Nottingham to Gatwick Airport. My old friend Dusty Jack, who was renowned for his many adventures to cultural sites, rang me from the States, telling me to have a safe trip and to make sure I told him all about it when I returned. I told him I would, but I didn't think my journey would be half as adventurous as those he was used to. Dusty would jump in where angels feared to tread and get into all sorts of bother. But it didn't seem to faze him at all.

The children woke to see me off and I waved them good-bye. Rush hour traffic was bad around London, making the time around 9:30 when I reached Gatwick. By the time the luggage had been checked in, it was time to set off to the boarding gate. In little to no time I was settled on the British Airways plane, picking up speed down the runway. I looked out the window as the plane left the ground, watching the people, the cars, and the houses becoming smaller as we gained height, and everything disappeared into oblivion. How insignificant we are within the vastness of our universe, I thought. A few miles up and even the landscape began to disappear from view.

As we reached our altitude above the clouds, the shapes they formed looked like heavenly cities in the sky, holding their own landscapes with sloping cliffs sweeping down to rippling seas.

The Journey

The flight to Kingston was to take about ten hours. I was due to reach Kingston at 3:30 Jamaican time.

The time passed quickly. I chatted to Myrtle, a lady in her seventies who grew up in Jamaica but had lived in England for the last forty years. She was going home to visit family, planning to spend two months there. She told me she would love to stay in Jamaica, spending her remaining years there until she died, but with all her children living in England, the way of life in Jamaica would be too hard for her alone. She thought this may be her last visit to the island.

She told me of the way things used to be back in her childhood days in her homeland, and she wondered how things might have changed since she had left all those years ago. It was in the '60s when Myrtle had arrived as a young woman to England. She told me how frightened she had been coming to a strange new land to make a new life for herself. She was going to live with her uncle, who was going to find her work in London. She told me how cold she had felt compared to the tropical climate she had come from and how dark and strange everything had looked within the grey, concrete surroundings. How the tall buildings had seemed to tower above her, and how the houses all had chimneys on their roofs. The people, too, seemed daunting, staring at her as though she were an alien. But settling into her

Through Crystal Clear Waters

new home in Brixton, time soon passed. She met a young Jamaican man at work, and a couple of years later they married. Working and making a life for themselves took up most of their time and money. The wages were a lot higher in England, but so were the bills. Every month, both she and her husband sent money home to their parents, along with letters stating their intention to come home one day. But that day never came. She brought up four children and got them through college and into jobs. There was never any time to take a trip to Jamaica. As time passed, her parents died, and fifteen years ago her husband passed away. All that was left in Jamaica were some cousins, who she was now going to see some forty-odd years after leaving home. I couldn't help feeling slightly sorry for this old lady who, whilst struggling to do what was right, somehow life had passed by. She had become trapped by a decision made forty years ago, and she had put her dreams on hold until her last years. Soon we were making our descent, the great plane thundering down the runway. I was looking forward to being able to get out and stretch my legs. As the doors opened and I put my foot onto the steps leading down to the tarmac, the intense climate of this Caribbean country hit me. The hot air blasting at me was like standing in front of an oven door.

The Journey

I accompanied Myrtle through passport control, which seemed to take ages, and helped her find her luggage. After we had both picked up our suitcases, Myrtle told me I was a very special person, and said she was sure I would find out who I realy was whilst in Jamaica, she also urged me to be careful of who I could trust on my next journey abroad. This puzzled me, what did she mean by who I realy was? I had not spoken to her of my having no 'roots' and I had no plans for another journey, so why the warning? She did make me realise though, that I too put-off the things I wanted to do, whilst going about the day to day things in life, and I should not leave things until it was too late. We bid each other good-bye and went our separate ways through the next round of customs-checking and paper-stamping.

Eventually I arrived outside the Kingston airport. I was hot, tired, and gasping for a cigarette. I walked down a wire-fenced walkway, looking at all the faces on the other side of it. There were hundreds of people searching for friends and relations they had come to collect from the queues of people leaving the airport. I was looking for Eli, a friend from college in Nottingham, and his sister Mary, who had come to pick me up. I was going to stay for a months vacation at their home in the heart of the country, high on a hilltop at Crooked River in Clarendon.

Through Crystal Clear Waters

Suddenly, I heard someone shout, "Hey, Chiane!" and looked across to see Eli and Mary call me. I headed towards the entrance. They had a hired car waiting, and after smoking a cigarette, we soon set off on another three-hour journey to Crooked River top.

The time was now about 5:00 p.m. and the traffic in Kingston was as congested as any British city as people left work at the factories. As we drove, people stopped and stared at the "white woman" passing by in the car. It amused me to think that back home in England, I was considered to be foreign-looking.

In a short time, we were out of Kingston heading up to the country. Jamaica was one of the largest islands in the Caribbean, and the roads were winding into the mountains. The drivers went at breakneck speed and behaved like maniacs, beeping their horns as they came to corners or when one car wanted to pass another. I didn't believe I could ever drive a car here in Jamaica.

I watched as we passed huge mountainsides and deep valleys, all covered in rich vegetation. I gazed on the rock face where they had carved out the roads in the mountains. Some of them were rough, where the Rock Springs had run gullies like small rivers down the hills, tearing up the roads, leaving big potholes and scattering rocks, so many that I thought they

The Journey

would surely stop the car in its tracks. But drivers were used to that here and managed to manoeuvre their vehicles over and around the obstacles. At times I thought the bottom of the car would tear up as we bounced over the rocks, scraping the chassis.

In some of the residential areas were large, pretty houses with large verandas, supporting electricity and water. Some were two stories high, surrounded by white-painted walls and fancy-styled wrought iron gates. But the further into the country we drove, the smaller the houses became—still neat in appearance, painted white with red or blue trim. They had verandas and zinc roofs that gently sloped to catch the rainwater in large drum pans.

Little houses were scattered all about the hillsides, and I wondered how the people were able to reach them. Some of the poorer houses were built of nothing more than a few sheets of zinc and wood and didn't look as good as the garden sheds back home. But that is where they lived and they seemed to be happy.

On driving through Spanish Town, we passed a ghetto on the outskirts, where hundreds of people were living in nothing more than lean-tos, covered with pieces of blue plastic or sacking. It was a dirty-looking place, and I was told that if your car breaks down on that stretch of road, you would not be safe.

Through Crystal Clear *Waters*

"Never stop on this road," the hire car driver told me. "They would strip you naked and take your clothes, jewellery, and money. You would be lucky to escape with your life. Even if you went for help, by the time you got back, the car would be stripped and all the parts sold off for scrap."

By the time we left Spanish Town the light was starting to fade, as we climbed higher and higher up into the countryside. Sunset there was about 6:30 p.m., and we still had a good way to go before we reached our destination. At about 8:45 p.m. we reached Crooked River and started to climb up to the little house on the hilltop. The route was so rough that some cars would not even attempt it. But our driver expertly manoeuvred his way up the winding, steep, rocky track, crawling over the roughest bits and steering cleverly around the big water-gauged dips on his way to the top of the hill. All the way up, houses were scattered about. The ones at the bottom had water piped to their homes. But about halfway up, the main pipe stopped. This place was called Cross Pass. Everyone above that point had no water at their houses and had to fetch their water from the standpipe.

It was a little after 9:00 p.m. when I at last sighted the neat little white house. There Eli and Mary's brother Wilfred, (called Bee) sat waiting on the veranda. After settling in, unpacking my case, and drinking a cup

The Journey

of coffee, I decided to retire. It had been nineteen straight hours of travelling, and I was exhausted. It didn't take me long to drop asleep, full of enthusiasm to wake up in this tropical island.

Chapter 4

Island Life

At around 5:00 a.m., I awoke to the sounds of a cockerel crowing and donkeys braying. Looking out the window, I saw people already up and going about their business. There were men heading off into the bush with cutlasses in their hands, children running barefoot down the rocky road carrying containers to fetch water, and people leading donkeys and goats to graze.

I got up, put on my trainers, and went outside. I washed my face with the dew that was dripping from the zinc roof. The dew water was soft and refreshing, just like nature intended. I headed off down the yard to the back of the house to the toilet, which was built of zinc and wood and shaded by banana trees. With no sewerage systems in the heart of the country, the toilets here were constructed by digging a deep pit over which was built a concrete box, with a seat on top made of wood and a cover for the opening.

Through Crystal Clear *Waters*

After making a cup of coffee, I went to sit out on the veranda, which overlooked the roadway with houses dotted about, going down the hillside. Even though I was up on a hilltop, everywhere I looked I could see large mountains, green with vegetation all around. As one mountain sloped down, another rose up behind it, and below in the valleys was a thick mist.

At around 6:30 a.m., the sun began to rise over one of the highest mountains. I watched it spread its golden rays over everything, giving light and awakening all the rich green colours. I watched the mists in the valleys start to rise, taking their place in the sky. It seemed as though the clouds had come down at night to cover the sleeping Earth, just like a mother covers her child with a blanket to protect it from the cold night air until the warmth of the morning comes.

Soon, the men I had seen earlier heading off to the bush with cutlasses in their hands were returning, carrying huge hands of green bananas and large bags filled with oranges and small apple-looking vegetables called *chuchu*. Women with bowls on their heads were coming up the hill, heading for the river, which was approximately two miles away, to wash their clothes. I saw a man leading a donkey. Strapped on either side of its back were two large baskets full of yams and sugarcane, and three small children rode, too. Everyone that passed by the veranda raised their hands and shouted good morning, and I returned their greeting.

Music soon started to fill the air, coming from the houses all around, as the sun got hotter and hotter. Boys dressed in khaki suits and girls in pinafore dresses, wearing backpacks, headed off down the hill for school. Dogs lay sunning themselves on the road. Parakeets were flying southwards, huge brightly coloured butterflies were fluttering past, and small hummingbirds, Jamaica's national bird, hovered, pollinating the bright-red flowers of the Croatian bushes, which hedged the border around the house.

All around, as far as the eye could see, were trees and plants. There were cedar, ango, orange, lime, and grapefruit trees, along with coconut, breadfruit, plum and pear trees. Banana and sugarcane were also in abundance, along with all kinds of peppers, garden egg, and pumpkin. I pondered whether the Garden of Eden would have looked like this. This was truly nature at its best, and although the people here were poor in commercial terms, I could see why they called this a tropical paradise. As I took in all these sights on my first morning in the heart of the carribean, I could feel the exuberance of youth creeping back, vowing to myself I would not get trapped in the rat race of the west again, and an intention to travel.

Through Crystal Clear Waters

Mary had cooked a breakfast of callaloo, a sort of Jamaican spinach seasoned with onions and peppers, which I lapped up eagerly with a couple of slices of bread and a cup of coffee.

After breakfast I went for a walk to explore. Every house I passed, people would call out good morning. Along the roadside, donkeys, goats, and even the odd hog or two could be found tied to a root to graze.

As I went on towards the bush, I picked up a slim bamboo stick to help me climb the steep, rocky hillside. I climbed higher and higher until I came to a large precipice, where far below the Rio Minho River winded its way through the valley. The way down to the river was almost vertical, and I wondered how the women managed to get up and down the steep incline with bowls of washing on their heads. Amongst the shrubs and trees going down to the river were several well-trod pathways. With the help of my bamboo stick, I carefully made my way down. As I did so, the air became cooler as I lost sight of the vast landscapes. I was heading to a place called Santa about a mile or so down the river, where the women had gone earlier. Across the river, the bush seemed to turn into rocks. I carried along the pathway until I saw some of the women chatting whilst they washed their clothes in the clear water running swiftly over the stones. Over the other side, high up on the rock face, a small waterfall was springing cool, clear water over the rugged rocks. The water was coming from a natural spring high up in the mountain, channelled down in a gully until it gathered in a pool lower down, which then spilled over, forming the waterfall. I thought about getting over to the waterfall and filling some bottles to take home for my children to taste. But it had taken so long to get this far, and the attempt to fill bottles would be too exhausting before trekking the long way back. Whilst gazing at the waterfall, I noticed a young man sat on the rocks, he was smiling and waving, the other women paid him no mind, as if he was not there, but I waved back at him.

The women told me a good place to catch the Rio Minho was at a place called Kippets, about two miles by road from Crooked River. They also told me to wait and go back up with them, as it was not good to come down there on my own. Before long we were all heading back up to Crooked River top. When I got back, Eli was not too pleased that I had gone there alone; saying that if I had fallen or hurt my foot, no one would know I was there. He told me that the place was so desolate; no one would hear if I cried for help, and I could possibly die before anyone could reach me. So I promised not to go there alone again and set about making arrangements for someone to take me to Kippets.

Through Crystal Clear Waters

The next couple of days I relaxed, drank coconut water, and ate oranges and star apples. I sat on the veranda and sketched the scenes going on around me. By the end of the week, we were to take a trip into Frankfield to change my English sterling into Jamaican dollars and do some shopping.

Over the next week I took bus rides to Frankfield, Chapelton, and the largest town in that area, May Pen. The bus rides were adventures in themselves. Instead of running to catch a bus as you did in England, here, the bus driver and his mate called you to come on the bus and waited till you got down the road to squeeze you in. They packed people in like sardines and then travelled speedily to their destination, collecting the fares as people got off the bus. The windows of the buses were darkened to protect them from the sun, and the sound systems blasted out traditional Jamaican music. Most of the buses had colourful names across the top of their windscreens, like "Life Saver" or "Irie Man." The journeys taken on these buses became etched in my memory forever.

In the towns, some of the shops looked like a view from an old Western movie, made of concrete and board. Street vendors were along all the pavements, some in little wood-hut shops, not only in the towns, but also on the roads leading in, selling coconut, fruit, yams, and juice drinks. Sound systems blasted out

Island Life

reggae music all down the streets and people hustled, trying to make a dollar. Young men with cars were constantly asking me if I wanted a taxi home, while street vendors tried to get me to buy whatever they had to offer. People sat on the streets talking, some begging me for money and some just watching me, as if they had not seen a white person before. I thought I heard someone call my name, and looking around I saw what looked like the same young man that had waved at me across the river, he stood staring at me across the street, I asked Mary if she knew him, but by the time she turned to look, he had gone. I thought I just imagined he was looking at me, and it was just a trick of the mind. All types of people went about their business as the sun beat down. Old Rasta men walked about barefoot with old tattered clothes and dreadlocked hair, matted until it didn't look like hair at all. Some shouted and swore as if they had been smoking too much ganja.

The following day, we took a trip down to Milk River, hoping to go on the beach there, but a community of Rastas had captured the land on either side of the rugged road leading to the beach. This made it impossible to get out of the car and go into the sea; for fear that they would steal our clothes or take the wheels off our car. The driver refused to stop here and I felt upset that I would not dip my toes

Through Crystal Clear Waters

in the Caribbean Sea. So we returned to Milk River Bath, a spa with mineral water that sprung from the rocks and ran through the spa into the river. It cost one hundred dollars for fifteen minutes in the spa. We bought half an hour and were shown to a door. Within was like our own private little swimming pool, approximately six feet square, neatly tiled, with the mineral water flowing in from one side and out the other to the river. I stepped into the water, finding it warm and slightly salty to taste. The water was about chest-deep with plenty of room for two people to float about in.

Legend had it that Milk River Bath had healing properties. A long time ago, back in the days of slavery, a young slave had been beaten by his master, found the natural pool, and went in to bathe his wounds. When he stepped out of the pool, he found all his lash cuts had been healed. The slave went running back to his master, showed him how he had been healed, and also showed him the spa pool. From that day on, the slave's master fenced off the pool and proceeded to build the spa, running the spring water into several baths and charging people to use them. Some people said that since the slave owner turned the spa into a commercial enterprise, the water lost its healing properties. Healing powers or not, the spa certainly refreshed me, and the salt in the water actually healed the itchiness of the mosquito bites I had been plagued with over the past few days.

After coming out of the spa, we had something to eat and drink and went across the road to where the car was parked near the river. A man approached us and asked if we would like to feed the alligators, which we agreed to do, so we were taken to a woman who asked us to purchase some "chicken back." She then took us through a gate to the edge of the river where a small section had been fenced off, and she began to call the alligators. We watched in amazement as the woman called "come, come" several times, and very soon, what looked like pieces of driftwood came nearer to the edge of the river. All of a sudden, two large alligators climbed onto the riverbank, and the woman started to throw the chicken back pieces over the fence to feed them. When all the chicken pieces had finished, the alligators turned round and went back into the river and swam off. As we watched them swim away, I marvelled at the intelligence of these creatures that seemed to cash in on people's interest in them and get several free meals a day.

A place I would not be so keen to visit again was downtown Kingston. I had accompanied Bee and Mary to the city hospital. On the run into the city were all the island's largest companies, such as Wray and Nephew (rum producers), Lasco (food producers), Toyota,

Through Crystal Clear Waters

BMW, and many more. But on going into the downtown heart of the city, I had never seen so much poverty. The streets were dirty and littered with rubbish; the buildings looked like they had been built centuries ago and were desperately in need of repair. I noticed that a lot of the people in downtown Kingston looked dirty and hungry, some just sitting around, others trying to hustle for money. There did not seem to be the same friendliness I had found in the country. Some people were definitely unapproachable and aggressive. I didn't think I could find words to describe what I felt as we drove through the desperately deprived streets on our way to the hospital, but I do think it must have been a living hell for those who had to live there. I had read that Kingston and the ghetto areas of Spanish Town, just down the road, were the most dangerous, violent places in Jamaica. Amongst the poverty were the crime, drugs and guns, leaving no one feeling safe. I would definitely not have liked to walk through those streets and was glad of the safety of our vehicle. Our driver told me to keep my arm inside the transit van we were in, as people had been attacked for their watches and rings. The thieves would have no conscience about chopping my arm off to get them.

As we drove back to the country, I reflected on the many different levels of life on this island. To come to

Island Life

Jamaica as a tourist and go to places like Montego Bay or Ocho Rios, did not show the true Jamaica. These were just idealistic hideaways. Those in the richer areas, like uptown Kingston, the Manchester areas, and others scattered about, could live a good life, as long as they protected themselves from thieves and gunmen. Those who lived in the country led a simple existence but were happy, churchgoing people surrounded by fruits and vegetables and their animals. Although they were short of the material things of life, they still had a lot going for them. But those who lived in the hellholes of the inner cities and ghettos did not seem to have a hope in the world.

As I lay in bed that night, I thought about how in our fast, commercial lives in the West, masked by opulence, we did not have the time to see what was going on around us.

But human beings were the same the world over, much of what we were was hidden and could only be found when we stepped outside our comfortable lifestyles and opened our eyes. On this beautiful tropical island, it would be easy to see only what you wanted to see. But if you were to look beyond the paradise, you would see the many different facets of the human race. It was not Mother Earth that made humans like they were, but rather the nature of man himself.

Chapter 5

The Meeting

The following week I decided to do some more exploring in the countryside. I paid a taxi man to take me as far as he could up one of the highest mountains in Clarendon, called Bull Head Mountain. We set off quite early and got a good way up before it was impossible to go any farther in the car. The rest of the way, I went on foot. On reaching the top, I expected to see the same drop on the other side, but instead it gently sloped into the area of Red Hill and Kellets. So I headed off into the direction of Kellets, as I had been told there were some caves there.

All across the landscape, little houses were dotted about, even in what seemed the most inaccessible areas. The sun was getting hotter and hotter, and I was glad I had remembered to bring my flannel to mop the sweat from my brow. Nearly every Jamaican carried their "rag" with them and after the first couple of trips out in this tropical heat, I understood

Through Crystal Clear Waters

why. I also carried some oranges, a bottle of water, and a packet of biscuits to keep me going on my way. I reached Kellets around midday and after taking a rest decided to head off to the caves. It took about an hour to reach them and I was amazed to find how deep into the rocks some of the caves went. After exploring one of the caves, I worked my way further up and around, until I reached another cave mouth set further back into the hillside. There on a rock in front of the opening was a young man dressed in brown ragged trousers and a green string vest. He wasn't wearing any shoes and his long black hair fell down his back in neat dreadlocks. As I approached, the young man smiled.

"You made it then?" he asked.

I was surprised and said, "Pardon?"

The young man patted the stone next to where he was sitting, inviting me to sit down, and carried on speaking in a type of broken patois. "Me bin sit ere long time waiting fe you." I looked at him and asked what he meant, as he did not know me. "Me know you man, and you know me. Me is Isaac, and me great-great-granddaddy tell me fe wait fe you here. His name is Izacal!"

I was silent for a few moments. Was this the same young man who waved at me by the waterfall and and

The Meeting

stared at me in the town? Izacal was in my dreams—a figment of my imagination, perhaps—and way back in England, so how could this young man have tapped into my dreams?

As if reading my thoughts, Isaac went on to tell me, "Dreamtime is a way of talking to the ancients. Me granddaddy tell me he first met you when you three years old, and he get fe speak wiv you two months ago. Much water passed through the river since then, and I av bin sat ere waiting fe you to come."

I was amazed. I had never taken my dreams for granted, but this was becoming reality. I even wondered if I was dreaming right now.

I took out my bottle of water and offered Isaac a drink. He took a sip and handed it back, looking at me with a smile. "You need time fe think?" he asked in a joking sort of way.

"Well, it takes a bit of getting used to, you know," I replied.

Isaac stretched back on the rock and said, "Me know, but me av nuff tings fe tell you, affore you travel back foreign."

I thought back to my dream before coming here and remembered Izacal saying he would be with me, even though I wouldn't see him. He had said he would guide me, telling me I would find what I thought I had lost many years ago. Was this what Isaac was going to tell me?

Again, as if reading my mind, he said, "You av found what you think you lost already, the power fe see clearly, fe understand, and fe think clearly. As a child your mind was open, but dis existence cloud your mind and pollute de river of your thoughts. But now it time fe you learn de truth, an me av nuff tings to say. Come, let us walk."

I got up and followed Isaac into the cave, wondering what this "truth" was going to be. We didn't speak as we twisted and turned through the passageway of the cave. Then, as we turned round a bend, I could see daylight pouring in through an opening high up in the rock. Isaac told me to come and climbed up to the opening, offering me a hand to pull me up the incline. When we reached the opening, Isaac spread out his hand to gesture me to look upon the landscape.

It was truly magnificent, a rich green valley with fruit and palm trees. A pure, clear river wound its way through, with waterfalls pouring into it at regular intervals. The sun glistened on the water, looking like stars in the night sky. I saw many brightly coloured birds with long, flowing tail plumage behind them

The Meeting

flying all around. Although I had seen many fantastic landscapes on this island, none of them seemed to appear on the same scale as this one. The one thing I did notice was that there were no houses scattered about, like most places on the island, I asked Isaac why this was.

"Dis is de land before man get fe do what he do best: fight, kill, an destroy tings. Dis is de land of de ancients." As we made our way down to the river, Isaac went on to tell me of his great-great-grandfather, Izacal. "Many years ago, long before your Western civilisation, there was one great land mass de ancients called Turtle Island. It was one great expanse of land before what you fe call 'continental drift.' When de land first began to separate, different areas of land formed, such as Mu, Lemuria, and Atlantis. The people there built great empires and made calendars, guided by de stars and planets. Life was rich and good. These people were far more advanced than you believe humans to be at that time. This is because, as a race, humans had been doomed for extinction many years before. Early man kept all his genetic information in the cells of his brain. I believe you call that stage caveman existence; all this was in what you refer to as the 'cradle of mankind' deep in Africa.

"As man developed and gene information got bigger, so did de size of de human brain, and many humans

Through Crystal Clear Waters

died regularly in childbirth. But at dis time, people from another planet were looking for somewhere to establish, because of problems of their own. You see, Earth humans were de children of time; they were de least advanced of de thirteen stars or planets with human-like life forms living on them. Planet Earth's atmosphere was de most dense. Izacal's grandparents came from Sirius B, a star planet, or 'white dwarf' as you call it—similar to your own planet, with a dense atmosphere. Sirius B operates more within a sixth dimension, whereas here on Earth tings are within de third dimension. Things are more solid, so to speak. Anyway, they came here and split genes wiv de evolving humans, taking gene information an entwining it wiv their own in the two twisting strands you call DNA. This meant you didn't have to keep genetic information in your brains, and de human race was saved".

He explained the people from Sirius B did not need a body to support their human energy but can appear to take any form of life they want, from man to animal, fish or bird. So integrating and splicing through primitive mating was an easy task to undertake. As years passed, man evolved. Cro-Magnon man was formed and over time groups migrated through various regions, out of Africa. They started colonies all over the world, occasionally coming across other groups of evolving humans. The African descendants had been

The Meeting

evolving a lot quicker than those groups encountered outside the 'cradle.' These still remained pre-Cro-Magnon or earlier in their development, and so didn't intermix.

By the time the African migrants had reached Eurasia, they were what you call *Homo sapiens* in their development. The last group of non-Africans they encountered were Neanderthal. They were still in the Cro-Magnon stage but were evolving fast, using tools, and the two groups seemed to get along side-by-side. The splicing or mating was not successful, as it was many years since DNA had formed in that group of migrants, so the strength of that first coupling of humans and star travellers was not as strong when passed on only through humans. The only way they could produce offspring was through Neanderthal females and *Homo sapiens* males, so the Neanderthal gene has all but disappeared. Scientists still cannot explain this leap in mankind, and call it the 'missing link.'

Western scientists would never accept how this came to be, as it would question their whole belief that Earth has the only intelligent life upon it and man is only one step away from the creator, God.

Isaac looked at me and smiled, probably because he saw the confused look on my face.

Through Crystal Clear Waters

I had heard stories of Atlantis and had studied the account of the Dogon, a remote African tribe in Mali who told of their ancestors' encounters with aliens, three thousand years ago. They called these aliens *Nommo*, from the Sirius system, and said they had taught them about astrology, mathematics, and law. I remembered reading that in the mid-nineteenth century, scientists had discovered a second star behind the Dog Star, Sirius, which they called Sirius B and that had a dense atmosphere, just as the Dogon had said.

Isaac continued to explain how his ancestors built a great empire on Atlantis, with pyramids surrounded by vast moats, lined with a crystalline structure. They maintained a very good living for many years, but they got greedy. They captured more land across the sea, captured slaves, and looked down on the indigenous people, abusing them in their search for power. In the end, they tried to start war with people of the Greek islands. Mother Earth had enough and sent a huge tidal wave. Atlantis disappeared overnight, along with the cruelty their power held."

As we walked, Isaac told me how the rulers had become so obsessed with power; they failed to listen to the Star Keepers and Planet Trackers, their wise men who were supposed to advise them when to do things. Several people who were not pleased with

The Meeting

what their leaders were doing had formed groups. They foretold disaster and spread to the far corners of the Earth on sailing ships to Europe, Africa, Asia, and the Far East. Some had gone to South America, and after the catastrophe of Atlantis, sailed out to the few islands left remaining after the land mass had disappeared. These islands were the Caribbean islands, of which Jamaica is the largest.

Isaac then spoke of how those who had settled in Egypt and South America began to teach the people there, who saw them as gods. Soon great empires sprang up, with both places building pyramids in the alignment of the star structure of Orion's Belt. But those who settled in Jamaica lived a simple life, living off the land, without the power struggle that had led to the destruction of their civilisation.

He explained how the people who settled in Jamaica had lived happily in what they called the Yallows, until the Spanish and later the English came. These power-mad humans had claimed and carved up the land, shipping off the produce to their own countries. The land was raped and the people of the Yallows, along with the indigenous Arawak Indians, had no rights. Soon these foreigners started bringing in slaves from the west coast of Africa to work in the plantations. The slaves were beaten and treated like dogs until Christian missionaries, many years later, talked of the

Through Crystal Clear Waters

wrong that was being done, and the slaves began to revolt. After many years of hardship and pain, slavery was abolished.

Today, there was no slavery in Jamaica, but the legacy left behind had not had a good effect. As people travelled abroad to work and bring back luxuries from the West, the greed, hate and bad mind was growing in this country, too. Drugs also had a big part to play in the road to destruction, with huge amounts of money changing hands in drug trafficking from country to country, while illicit substances controlled the mind of the population and destroyed the human spirit. Violence was in the cities and spreading islandwide, doing what humans did best— destroying what they have.

I felt sad; the truth was that whenever a country was on top and prosperous, it seemed to look down on those not so advanced. They would claim others' land for their own, killing anyone who tried to stop them or robbing them of their heritage by assimilation, forbidding them to use their own language or practice their own religion. I felt ashamed to be a member of the human race. If this is what we had come to, what would the future hold?

"Come, time fe go," Isaac called out as he made his way to the cave entrance.

The Meeting

"But wait," I cried. "You can't end it there. I need to know more."

Isaac smiled and said, returning to his broken patois, "Tis nuff fe now. Me soon cum talk wiv you, but fe now go home and sleep."

On coming back out of the cave mouth and making my way back to Kellets, I turned to wave to Isaac, but he had gone. I reached Crooked River late in the evening, when the sun had gone down. I sat on the back step and gazed up at the stars, wondering when I would see Isaac again. Did I have to go all the way up Bull Head Mountain again? If I did, would he be there? I felt mad at myself for not asking him when we could meet, but something told me it didn't matter. I knew I would see him when the time was right. So I retired to bed and hoped to dream.

Chapter 6

The Gift

The next few days passed. Apart from making a trip to Frankfield, I just took walks around the yard, took photos, made sketches, and sat back, eating oranges and drinking coconut water. Mary was a good cook and each evening prepared a feast of beef, chicken, or fish, accompanied by rice and peas or yam and potatoes, with callaloo or cabbage.

For several days there had not been any rain. I had been rubbing white rum on my mosquito bites and every morning had woken up with more bumps on my legs. They were driving me mad with the itching. In fact, I believe I had used more white rum on my bites than I had been drinking.

I liked white rum. I would drink it with either "eggnog" or as a rum punch, with tropical fruit juice and ice cubes. I did not watch much television, even though it was often on in the living room. Every night I would sit out on the veranda with Eli, Bee, and Mary, and we would chat the night away. Sometimes we would take

Through Crystal Clear Waters

walks down to Cross Pass, where the young men and boys would play football while the girls watched, or Eli would catch up with friends he had not seen for many years, reminiscing on their verandas. Everyone was very friendly and it was interesting listening to their conversations of the past. Some of the men would sit outside the bars drinking their white rum, laughing and chatting, and most of the time music could be heard drifting out over the hilltops and valleys.

Electricity was in the majority of the houses here, brought to the houses by wires on poles, just like our telephone poles in England. Cooking was done on Calor gas stoves in the kitchen, or barbecues outside. Several people had mobile phones, so modernisation was here in this remote part of the country.

Children could be seen playing on the rocky road with toys they had made for themselves, like a tin lid on a piece of stick that they would run along the road with, or they would make a net ball post out of a stick and a plastic crate from one of the shops and practise shooting hoops. Usually the children would play barefoot to save their shoes for school or church.

We would get a taxi to fetch water in large containers, usually from the crossroads when we came back from shopping. But some of the younger people could be seen carrying containers to their houses on

The Gift

their heads after walking for up to a mile to reach the standpipe. When I wanted to take a bath, I would fill a tin bath from the water butt in the morning, leave it out in the sun to warm it up, and then get Eli to help me carry it into the bathroom. It was well worth the effort though, as the rainwater was soft and clear, just like the morning dew, and left my skin feeling fresh and silky.

One morning in the third week of my stay, I put some bun and cheese and a bottle of cola champagne into a bag and set off down the sloping pathway and up the hill to the area of Bray Head. With several stops on the way to rest, I made it to the top just before midday. As I stood and looked down towards Crooked River, I saw a figure climbing up towards me. As he came closer, I saw the familiar face of Isaac, smiling and waving at me. I was happy to see him and wondered what he was going to tell me this time. When he reached the top, he sat down beside me, put his hand in his pocket, and pulled out something wrapped in a cloth, which he stretched out his hand and gave to me. "Me bring sumting fe you," he said.

I took the bundle and carefully opened it up to find a long wand like piece of quartz crystal. I held it up to the sunlight, and as the sun glistened through this magnificent piece, it captured all the colours of the rainbow. I could see it was a flawless piece of crystal.

Through Crystal Clear Waters

"It's beautiful," I said as I gazed at its perfect form. I had several small pieces back home and had long been interested in this precious, timeless rock. I had quite a collection of precious stones, including malachite, amethyst, tourmaline, and slices of amber, but none were as beautiful as this piece.

"Me know you did like dem," Isaac told me. "And dis one special, you know. It fe help you dream, and tis full of information."

I thanked Isaac for the crystal and told him how I had searched many places to find the bits of crystal I had at home. I had visited Matlock in England, where there were many precious rocks and stone on sale from all over the world. I had been to a place called the Heights of Abraham and gone deep into the caves there. I had heard about the healing properties of crystal; how it could help you get your body in balance and improve your concentration. I kept a piece of quartz crystal under my pillow to try to help improve my dreams. Crystal was even being used in the modern computer world. At the heart of every computer was a piece of quartz crystal that could store information. Scientists were now able to make crystal, but first they needed a natural piece of quartz to "breed" them.

I told Isaac what I knew of the legends of crystals, how the Indians of America treasured them, believing them

The Gift

to be gifts from the gods and capable of prophesying the future. There was a book entitled *The Mystery of the Crystal Skulls* that stated that hidden in many parts of the world were thirteen crystal skulls, said to contain all the information of the universe, past, present, and future. These skulls were said to have been fashioned by thought by non-human forms, with no evidence of craftsmanship.

Isaac listened intently, then laughed, saying, "Me see you av bin doing your homework as dey say, so me think you won't av much problem wiv what me av fe tell you." We sat down and I shared my bun and cheese with Isaac before he told me his next story.

Chapter 7

The Ancients

Talking in his usual patois, he began: "Me ancestral grandfather, Izacal, was a Star Keeper and Planet Tracker, what you may call a high priest or shaman. When Atlantis was being built into a great empire, Izacal was a small boy. His father was learning to be a Star Keeper from his father, Izacal's grandfather. Da role of Star Keepers and Planet Trackers was handed down from father to son, and their job was fe keep records and advise leaders of right times fe build, plant crops and make new laws, in accordance with what da stars and planets' positions commanded. They understood every ting was connected—da universe, galaxies, planets including Earth, and da stars. Every ting was reliant on each other—sea, wind, plants, animals, and humans, were all part of one living thing."

He went on to explain, "Things that happen on one side of da universe will affect things on da other side. Imagine an asteroid colliding wiv one of da planets in your galaxy—let's say da one you fe call Pluto. You wouldn't think it have any significance fe you here on Earth, but it does, like a change of climate affecting nature. Likewise, if da people here on Earth keep tearing down rainforests and killing off animal species, it fe have a knock-on effect somewhere else in da universe, cuz everyting is connected. Do you understand?"

I nodded, and Isaac went on to tell me how his ancestors' leaders became greedy, wanting control of other landmasses, attacking and claiming land. Sometimes when they went to other lands where the people were of darker skin, those people saw these fairer-skinned Atlanteans, with their advanced skills and often thought them to be gods. This led to a sort of supremacy of the Atlantean leaders, who forgot about their connection to everything and only about their own power. They lost respect for the order of things and began to think that they themselves controlled the planets and the stars. They started killing and taking slaves to build in their own land, treating them worse than beasts of burden.

When the Star Keepers and Planet Trackers warned them about their actions, the leaders became angry and locked them away so they could not interfere with their plans. Izacal's grandfather was locked away, and his son, Izacal's father, who should have become

The Ancients

Star Keeper after his father's death, began to meet in secret with others to consult the calendars and keep records. They stopped writing down records on the stone tablets but transformed all the information into selected pieces of crystal. This was done by thought, through a state of trance and concentration. When all had been recorded into the crystals, they were divided up between the twelve Star Keepers and Planet Trackers, who made plans to take them to the far corners of the Earth, before the consequences of their leaders would bring about the catastrophe they had foreseen. Each of the crystals held a part of the records—of things that had happened from the beginning of time, of things that were happening at that time, to things that were to come. To put all the information into one crystal would have been too dangerous.

They then gathered their families and followers and after destroying all the stone records, written in hieroglyphs in the Atlantis pyramids, set sail one night in twelve boats while the leaders were sleeping. After bidding each other good-bye, they travelled off in twelve different directions, knowing they would never meet again in their lifetimes.

They remained connected by thought and could communicate with each other through dreamtime. They became nomads until they found land where they could build their tribes. And so it was that the twelve tribes scattered over the Earth, each taking their piece of crystal information. Our own Christian Bible even made reference to the twelve tribes.

Isaac concluded his story by telling me, "Over time some tried fe build empires again wiv da indigenous people they lived amongst, such as in Egypt and South America. You can still see today where they built fe them empires, as it is where you find pyramids. But each time an empire was built, da same thing happened after time. Greed, slavery, and killing. Ultimately da empires fell, not in de same way as Atlantis, which disappeared from Earth in no more than a day and night, but simply by their own greed, or by de opposition of people from other lands who were becoming advanced themselves.

"Other tribes did not try to build empires, as they could see da destruction it caused, but instead blended in with da communities where they settled. They taught in subtle ways, without dramatically changing lifestyles. Izacal became Star Keeper in dis island you fe call Jamaica, and his tribe mixed wiv da Arawak Indians and wiv a tribe called da Taíno dat lived here. The Taíno were a farming, fishing, and hunting community that had migrated from the Orinoco Basin about AD 650. They cultivated cassava, which they made into bread called *bammy*. They

The Ancients

cooked meat over a fire on a four-legged stand called a *bucan*, made of spiced wood called pimento. They lived together happily fe many years till da European invasion. Me is now da Star Keeper and da Holder of da crystal."

All this was a lot to absorb, and soon it was time to be heading back to Crooked River. Isaac said he would meet with me one more time before I went back to England, and we went our separate ways once again.

Chapter 8

The Crystal

I reached Crooked River top just before dark and sat on the bed looking at the piece of crystal Isaac had given me. As I held it in my hand I could feel warmth emanating from it and was puzzled as to where Isaac had found such a beautiful piece. As far as I could find out, no one knew of anywhere in Jamaica that crystal could be found.

I wondered what the piece of crystal looked like that had been handed down to Isaac, who was now the Star Keeper. How big must it be and what information did it hold? Isaac had said it held information from the beginning of time through to the future, which seemed to me an incomprehensible amount of data and which must have needed a massive piece of crystal to store. He had told me that it had been divided into twelve separate pieces, which when brought together would contain the whole picture of events—past, present, and future.

Through Crystal Clear Waters

Did all twelve pieces come from one giant piece of crystal? When, if ever, would they all be brought together? What would happen if we were to have this information? Would things change? Would they improve? Would it alter our way of thinking? There were so many questions.

Isaac had said the information had been separated because it would be too dangerous to keep in one place. What did he mean by dangerous? Who would it endanger? I wondered how anyone could extract such a huge amount of information from the crystal. Did Isaac know how to get the data from his piece? Could he update it as to what was happening in the present? Question after question spun round in my head, making me feel tired, so I resigned myself to asking Isaac the next time I saw him.

The last three weeks had really sped by in Jamaica; I only had one week left. With all I had been told and the many questions I needed to ask, I wondered if I would be any wiser when I reached home. Every time I learnt anything, it always posed many questions, leaving me with the opinion that in this life, there are more questions than answers. With that thought in mind, I put my crystal under my pillow and closed my eyes. Sleep soon came.

The Crystal

I dreamt I was in a huge valley, surrounded by massive rocks; in fact it was more like a canyon. It definitely was not Jamaica; the area was barren, like a desert. I seemed to be at some sort of convention, with thousands of people from all over the world, gathered in groups, talking. I saw American Indians, each in their brightly coloured tribal costumes. I could distinguish about ten different races from around the world, including African, South Asian, and Chinese, all in traditional costume. I also saw a group of Tibetan monks talking to some Arabs. There was a large group of Mexicans, dressed in long white robes with red sashes, all wearing sombreros; there were Egyptians and Bedouins. There were also Westerners, with the men dressed in white shirts and grey trousers, and the women in colourful summer dresses and sandals. It seemed that every nation in the world was represented there.

As I looked around, I spotted Isaac, who was wearing a short white toga with a gold braid round his waist. He was talking to a small group who were dressed the same way he was.

As I watched intently at what seemed to be a world convention, a large conch horn sounded and echoed around the canyon. Everyone started heading off in the same direction, so I followed. They all gathered around a huge, flat-topped rock, forming a gigantic

Through Crystal Clear Waters

circle. There was silence. Not one person spoke, and as the sun passed exactly overhead, casting no shadow from the rock, the conch horn sounded again. At the sound of the horn, several people came out of the crowd circle, in towards the rock. I noticed Isaac was one of those people; he was carrying a bundle about the size of a football. I counted another eleven people from different nations, each carrying a similar bundle. They each climbed on top of the flat-topped rock and formed a circle, facing out towards the crowd, just like the numbers on the face of a clock. They all raised their bundles above their heads and the whole surrounding crowd cheered and clapped.

The conch horn sounded again, and the twelve on the rock started to unwrap their bundles while the crowd looked on in silence. It soon became apparent that each of the bundles held a large piece of crystal, and as they each held them high above their heads, the sun's rays hit the twelve crystals, sending out rainbow-coloured beams of light, upwards and outwards, forming a crown above the rock.

It was truly breathtaking; it made me want to cry. Not one word was spoken while all this was going on, but I could hear a low hum, almost like interference from a radio. As I listened, I discerned it was coming from the crystals. Soon the noise became louder. As it did, the whole crowd started to hum along with the crystals, until the whole canyon echoed with this almost supernatural sound.

As the sun moved across the sky, and the shadow of the rock started to return, the twelve wrapped back the crystals in the bundles they had carried them in and returned to their groups in the crowd.

A Cherokee chief came forward and stood on the rock. He was wearing a long parchment-coloured robe and a headdress of brightly coloured feathers, braids, and beads, which trailed all the way down his back. He was about sixty, with many lifelines etched over his face, a strong jaw, and large bright eyes like those of an eagle.

He raised both his hands to the sky as he walked around the top of the rock, before addressing the crowd. He greeted the people and thanked them for being there, paying tribute to the twelve Star Keepers and Planet Trackers; guardians of the crystals. He then went on to say, "The ancients spoke of a time to come when the people of Mother Earth would gather together from every corner of the globe to begin to uncover the truth. Time here on Mother Earth has seen the guardians having to hide the truth, for fear of the power being misused as it has been many times before—used to destroy all the Creator has formed."

Through Crystal Clear Waters

He continued. "The children of Mother Earth were too young to hold this knowledge, and much time had to pass before this day could come. Now the children of Mother Earth have grown. They control the air, the seas, and the land. They seek what is on the other planets, trying to control the heavens. People here are becoming as advanced as the ancients, and a new cycle is about to begin. The power that the people of Mother Earth have is not being put to good use, and it is now time for us, the Star Children and descendants of the ancients, to meet. We must prepare to make the whole world see and hear the information so they do not make the mistakes they are heading for, which would mean certain destruction for Mother Earth.

"It is us, the Star Children, whose duty it is to awaken the world, so we can see the sun rise on the new cycle, and everything will be in balance again."

Everyone started cheering, but just as another person was preparing to speak, I woke up.

I was upset, as I wanted to know what happened next. Then, as I rubbed my eyes, a light caught my attention. It was the piece of crystal Isaac had given me; it had slipped out from under my pillow and was emitting a white light, seemingly reflecting the moonlight.

The Crystal

As I gazed at it, I could hear a faint humming sound, just like when I was dreaming.

Had the crystal given me this truly amazing dream? I wondered. Why had Izacal and Isaac contacted me and what did they want? Where did I fit in with all this?

* * *

Friday, only left me four more days in Jamaica before I had to fly home. I knew I had to meet up with Isaac before I left. I really needed some answers, and only he could give them, I was sure of that.

I decided to hold my crystal and think about Isaac, in the hope that he would somehow hear me. I was beginning to panic and would try anything, no matter how farfetched it seemed, to talk with Isaac again.

Chapter 9

Mankind Drowning

Saturday morning came and I awoke early, around 3:00 a.m., and just could not get back to sleep. It was still dark as I looked out the window and I lay down, but there was a kind of restlessness creeping up on me. I decided to go outside.

The night sky was clear and so near up here on the hilltop. Everything was quiet and peaceful. When evening came in Jamaica, a whole new sound filled the air. I would hear crickets and bullfrogs, and the whole place was alive with noise. As it grew darker, bright lights became visible as the *peenies*, or fireflies, flew about, looking like tiny stars coming down from the heavens to check on nature as it fell asleep. But for now, everything was still and quiet, the whole world seemed to be sleeping—except me.

I was fascinated by the patterns the stars made as they flickered up above me. I could see many of the constellations clearly. I thought the stars were trying to tell me something as they twinkled, as if speaking in some sort of code.

I thought I must be going mad, thinking I could communicate with crystals and stars. But things had not been exactly normal since starting out on this trip, and it had gotten even crazier over the last few weeks. I thought that if I were to tell people of all I had seen and heard, they would definitely think I had lost the plot.

As the light began to creep over the mountains, I knew the sun would soon be coming up. I had stayed outside watching the night sky for at least two hours. It did a whole load of good, because I no longer felt restless; in fact, a tranquil attitude had taken over, as if there was no urgency in anything, and I felt at peace. I made a cup of coffee and sat out on the veranda to watch the sun rise.

As it woke and warmed the Earth, I tried to make sense of it all. I thought about what was going on all over the world; how people treated one another. I remembered the dreadful pictures on television of wars in Africa, Afghanistan, and Palestine. The terrible scenes of suicide bombers, hijacked planes flown into the Twin Towers in America, and all the devastation these had caused. How America and Britain, backed by many other countries, had retaliated by waging war on terrorists. The headlines now concentrated

Mankind Drowning

on President Bush's plans to bring down terrorism in seven different countries, and how Britain's prime minister, Mr Blair, was going to back him, starting with a war on Saddam Hussein.

I reflected on the crime levels rising in almost every country, of the accusations against political leaders, of unlawful practises and profiteering. Of starvation in third-world countries, while huge companies continue to rip people off in search of bigger profits while their directors awarded themselves gigantic pay rises. I thought of places that didn't have basic services like water or shelter, of the slums all over the world—how the street children in Colombia, considered no better than rats, were rounded up and killed. Drug barons made millions trafficking and destroying lives. The numbers of people shot on our streets rose by the year amid gang warfare.

Even the medical world didn't seem to have any conscience. Waiting lists got bigger and people continued to suffer. Scientists spent millions manipulating genes, cloning animals, and creating laboratory babies. Disease took its toll in ever increasing numbers, the biggest threat being AIDS. It was almost like twentieth-century leprosy, yet our streets were filled with young single mothers. The Christian faiths didn't go without blame either; Catholic priests were facing prosecution for molesting children. In fact, the majority of wars were fought in the name of religion.

It all made me wonder who we could turn to for support and salvation, let alone who we could trust. Humans, as advanced as we may have been, didn't seem very happy. The more we prospered, the more we seemed to destroy.

Then again, not all mankind was tarred with the same brush. I thought about Live Aid, where all the pop stars got together to raise money for the third world, and everyone rallied round to support them. Charities like Oxfam and World Vision didn't just send money but went to the areas in need to make a real difference. Images of hunger and starvation on television inspired thousands of people to put their hands in their pockets, with tears in their eyes and pain in their hearts at the sight of such suffering. Every year, Children in Need collected millions of pounds for orphans and poor children all over the world, with film stars, comediennes, singers, and celebrities giving their time to appeal for their plights. Plus, there were always missionaries and other people who went out of their way to make a difference, sometimes at the risk of their own lives. Even in times of disaster, people forgot about their own safety and ran to the assistance of others. When floods, hurricanes, tsunamis, earthquakes, or volcanoes devastated and wreaked havoc, the community spirit crept back in to help.

So there was hope for mankind yet, I thought. All was not lost. All we needed to do was maintain that community spirit and kindness all the time, not just when disaster struck. We needed to respect each other, respect nature, and respect our planet.

The universe itself had sent many signs concerning the end of the era of Pisces, to usher us into the new era of Aquarius. Scientist and astrogers tell us of the Hale-Bopp comet, the total eclipse, and the spectacular sights of asteroids exploding into Jupiter. Nature also had its signs—we see reports on television of climate changes, El Niño, floods, and storms in places we would not expect. Scientists warned of a hole in the ozone layer and shifting polar caps. Yet we still didn't see the need to change our views and look after life on Earth.

Suddenly, all that Isaac had told me and what I had seen in my dream now made sense. It appeared that mankind only started to repair things when we reach our lowest. Every era threatened to be our last, but somehow we managed to pick ourselves up—only to start our path to destruction again and again. They say the darkest hour is just before the dawn, and I thought to myself just how true this was.

Through Crystal Clear Waters

I turned the radio on and a preacher was talking. He told a story that summed up all I had been analysing, about a man who was drowning in a river. On the riverbank were two men, one who couldn't swim and the other an expert swimmer.

The non-swimmer called to the other man, "See? The man is drowning! You must jump in and save him." The expert swimmer just stood watching the drowning man. The first man called out again, "Are you deaf? You can save him, why don't you jump in?" The swimmer still stood motionless. The first man called out a third time, "Have you no heart? The man is dying."

The swimmer, after a few seconds, dived in just as the man in the water was about to go under, pulling him to the riverbank and saving his life.

The first man came over to the swimmer and asked him why he had waited until the drowning man had almost lost his life before saving him.

The swimmer replied, "If I had dived straight in, he would have drowned us both. I waited until he had lost his strength. Only then could I bring him to safety."

I wondered if the people of Earth had lost enough strength to be saved. When was the right time to

Mankind Drowning

save mankind from drowning? What was our future? Would God save us? Would our creator give us yet another chance?

I decided to do some sketching for the rest of the day. Tomorrow, Sunday, I was going to make a trip to an old cane mill to see how they used to extract the juice from the sugarcane before modern times. One of the local men, Andy, had invited Eli and me to go with him to Morgan's Hill. They had restored an old mill and were going to extract some juice, which I was going to taste. I was looking forward to it.

As I sat sketching in the shade under a tree, a large brown lizard sat on a log next to me. I stopped sketching and watched the lizard, which was looking at me intently. As I watched, its colour changed from brown to green, with shades of red and blue on its underbelly and tail. The lizard came closer and closer, so I decided to sketch it. Just as I had captured its form, it ran straight across me and up the tree.

Soon after, a group of local children came over and started a conversation with me, asking about England, if I had children, and how long I was staying in Jamaica. I thought about how the children in Jamaica had very few toys to play with, and what they did have they made for themselves. But I had never seen them quarrel or fight, and they always looked after the younger ones, sharing what they had. It was something I rarely saw in the opulent West.

Chapter 10

Summing Up

Sunday came. I made my coffee and sat on the veranda, watching as people went down the road, dressed in their Sunday best, heading off to church. Jamaica boasted a huge churchgoing population, with as many churches in any community as there were pubs in an English town. Although there were probably as many rum bars as there were churches, hardly any women visited them. Neither did I see many women smoking cigarettes. I must have been shocking many people with my twenty-a-day habit, but even if they disapproved of this cigarette-smoking woman who did not go to church and drank rum punch on the veranda in the evenings, they did not show it.

Everyone was used to me by now and always called out to me and waved or stopped and talked. One woman would even call out "Chiane!" if she didn't see me when she passed in the morning, and another invited me to her house to hold her new granddaughter, a cute, bright-eyed little bundle called Lekeisha, who was all of three weeks old. I had also formed friendships with some of the children, one in particular. He was a young boy I had first met when I had spent a week visiting Mary and Bee nine years before this trip. His name was Kendrick and had been only four years old at the time. I used to talk to him and give him sweets on the veranda, something about this young boy made me bond with him. He had cried when I left Crooked River to return to the tourist area of Ocho Rios. When I got home, I used to send money or gifts for Mary to give to Kendrick.

Now he was thirteen years old and didn't like school and so wouldn't attend. He spent most of his days helping men on their land or looking after the animals. I tried to persuade him to return to school, so as to have more chances of employment later, but I didn't think he would listen to my advice. He had trouble reading and writing and told me he would get angry when he couldn't do things and didn't like it when other children laughed.

I could relate to this, as although I didn't have any problems academically as a child, I still had trouble being accepted for whom I was, and this made the bond with Kendrick stronger. I would praise him for his qualities; he was very good at growing crops and had a wonderful way with animals. He told me he also had dreamtime friends and often relayed his dreams to me. He got quite excited when telling me about a dream he had about meeting me, in a foreign country when he was a man. He said we were with a group of people all there to do the same thing, to collect information for a new world, and was happy about the fact that he didn't have to read or write, also that everyone felt like family. I told him I considered him as family, and was sure I would see him again in the future.

Sunday afternoon, I was all set to go with Eli to Morgan's Hill to the cane mill. Andy arrived to take us up there, and I was surprised to find out we were going there on foot. Off we went, heading off in the same direction as the women took to go to the river. But instead of going down to the riverbank, we kept to the high path onwards and upwards until we reached Morgan's Hill. The whole trek took about an hour, and we were very hot in the afternoon sun by the time we got there.

We prepared to juice the cane. Andy fetched a large bucket and a clean cloth from a house that used to belong to his family, although no one lived there now. Andy used the house when he was working the mill, which was situated at the back of the house, shaded by banana trees and coconut palms. The mill itself was a large metal encasement, mounted on a wood and bamboo platform. It contained three metal grinding drums, the largest of which protruded through the top of the encasement and had a long log chained to the top of it. The large drum drove the two smaller drums by a network of cogs, with a spout to drain the juice between the two small drums. Originally the whole thing would have been worked by a couple of donkeys tied to either end of the log to turn the large drum. The mill was built in the '40s, and on the encasement I could determine the words "Chattanooga, Tennessee, USA."

Andy placed the bucket under the spout and tied the cloth loosely over the top to filter the trash from the juice. He prepared a dozen or so pieces of sugar cane, cutting them to size, and splitting one end he placed a ginger root in the split, explaining that this improved the flavour of the juice.

Having no donkeys, we were to take turns pushing the logs round to work the mill, two of us pushing while the third fed the cane through the mill. Andy started to feed the cane while Eli and I ran round and round the mill, pushing the log turning the grinding drum to extract the juice. It was very hard work, and even though the area was shaded, it was still very hot and we were certainly building up a sweat. It seemed to

Summing Up

take ages to grind all the cane and I was exhausted. A couple of men, Kevin and Clive, came to help as they waited to juice their cane, and I took a well-earned rest.

Andy took the cloth off the top of the bucket and started pouring the juice into plastic bottles. The juice looked like dirty water, not very much like something you would want to drink, but I was hot, tired, and very thirsty, so I did not refuse when Andy passed me a bottle to take my first taste. It was cool and refreshing, tasting rather like a flat ginger beer. We sat talking and drinking the cane juice and taking in turns helping Kevin and Clive work the mill. When we were all finished, we set off back down the hill home, carrying our bottles of cane juice. The men were joking about how strong the white woman from England was and said they gave me "nuff respect!," which I took as a compliment. When we got back to Mary and Bee's house, Bee nearly fell off his chair laughing, telling me my face was as red as a bee sting. But we all enjoyed drinking the juice and there was enough left to put in the fridge for tomorrow.

The next day, Monday, was the last free day I had. Tuesday I planned to go to May Pen with Mary to buy some gifts to take home to the children and to go to the fish market for our last supper before I flew home.

Through Crystal Clear Waters

So I had to make the most of Monday. I took up my stick and set off early in the morning. I decided to take the route down to Santa, even though everyone had advised me not to. But I was going to take the footpath round the other side of the river, to the rocks where the waterfall was. I thought that route to be safe enough and I knew I would be strong enough to manage it on my own.

When I got there, I sat down on the rocks and watched the river flowing swiftly past. It was so peaceful there; I picked up a few stones and started to throw them down into the water. As I did, I heard a voice from behind me saying, "Is you bored, fe throw dem stones so?"

I looked round and saw Isaac, making his way down the rocks toward me. "No, I am not bored, I was just thinking," I replied. As he approached, I told him I had been worried I would not see him again, as I had so many questions to ask him.

Isaac just laughed and told me I worried too much, that he had told me we would meet again, and that I was letting my Western urgency creep back in. "Relax, man!" he said and beckoned me to follow him back up the rocks. We walked in the direction of Trout Hall. When reaching the shade of some trees, Isaac told me to sit under a big gwango tree and wait for him. "Soon come," he said as he took up his cutlass and ran over to a large coconut tree.

I watched as he expertly ascended the tree, repeatedly gripping it with both hands and pulling his bare feet up towards his hands, his cutlass gripped firmly between his teeth. He threw down two water coconuts, descended the tree, and brought them back to where I was sitting. He sliced off the top of one with a swing of his cutlass, cut a hole in it, and passed it to me to drink. As usual on this tropical island, the day was hot and this delicious drink was just what the doctor ordered. After I had finished drinking, Isaac split the coconut in half, fashioned a spoon from the top he had cut off, so I could eat the sweet jelly inside the coconut. After we both had finished, Isaac stuck his cutlass in the ground and lay back under the tree. "You want fe know where you fit in?" he said, looking over at me.

"Yes," I said. "And what is to happen next? How can we change things and make the world see what they are doing? There must be more to life than this, and—"

"Stop, stop. Slow down," Isaac cut in as he looked up into the gwango tree and sighed, telling me that where there is hope there is a future, and there is still hope for Mother Earth. "You see," he said, "fe every action there's a reaction. Remember I told you events

Through Crystal Clear Waters

happening on Earth affects tings da other side of da universe. Well it's like that fe everything. People do bad tings and others see they are wrong and try to make a difference. They protest about cutting down rainforests and demonstrate until da authorities' compromise. When people see da plight of da third world, they form charities providing water, shelter, and medication. When disaster strikes a country, other countries send help and provisions. When communities are smashed by nature, like earthquakes or floods, even by war, da richer countries help build those communities up again. So there is hope."

Isaac went on to tell me that the time to make people listen is when things go wrong, and that time only comes round every so often, at the time of Renewal. Those things had to be so bad that people would sit up and take notice. It is then that they realise that people starving in Africa or a war in the Middle East will inevitably affect them. He explained that someone sitting in front of their television, thinking of buying a bigger, better dining room suite, and would not see the images of the rainforest being destroyed. They would think it didn't affect them because they didn't live there, but it did. When they opened their eyes, they would realise those actions affected us all.

That time would soon be here, he said. Every time the planets returned to their beginnings, a new era began.

Summing Up

Every era had a name, and this would be the Age of Aquarius, People would open their eyes and see what was happening, understanding that it would affect them, their children, and their children's children.

At the beginning of the new era, Isaac explained, signs and wonders would be seen in the heavens and on Earth. Those who had faith and lived in hope would take notice, but those who did not care for anything but their own personal wants would ignore the signs. These people would perish, leaving those with hope with another chance to put things right. Without hope, without those people who wanted to make a difference and recognise that everything is connected, there would be no more chances on Mother Earth.

I told Isaac I understood, and he said he knew, that I had understood from an early age, but had got confused along the way and became unable to see clearly. It was his job to tell me where I fit in and help me see clearly again.

He said I was born into this Earth without a past, taken in by strangers until I was old enough to be independent. Yes, I had a mother and father I could not find, but instead of thinking about what was missing and about my lack of history and blood family, I should think more of having no chains binding me to a certain way of life. No roots meant there were no consequences. I had begun life with a clean slate so to speak, able to mould my own life by my own experiences. When people said I was different when I was young, it had made me strong, because I could see.

The ancients that came here, he said, were different; they blended with Earth's children and together formed future generations. All over the world lived the descendants of the ancients, and hidden deep in their genes were experiences of the Star Children and the ability to make a difference. There are also the 'chosen ones', called crystal children who will help people enter into this new age.

A new cycle would begin in the year 2012, and preparations were being made by the descendants of the twelve tribes to ensure we started the new era with a good foundation. This had been prophesied by humans since civilisations began—Mayans and their calendar, and the dawning of the Age of Aquarius and the new cycle of humanity.

Over the years we would see a lot of changes, both in nature and the balance of power in man. We would hear news of floods, earthquakes, and tsunamis in unexpected places. Of wars that would set the whole world at odds and of trouble in rich countries that would bleed them of their wealth, diminishing their

Summing Up

power. We would hear of people standing up against the power of their governments, of protests and riots. There would be diseases caused by scientifically altering crops, meat, and fish, rendering them poisonous to eat. But we would also hear of world leaders holding conference with the "little people," those that were once considered simple or uncivilised. Those that once oppressed them would seek their council.

At last, Isaac told me his job was done and that he had told me all he needed to say. It was now up to me to know what my part was, that he could not tell me. I must look within myself, find my talent, and use it.

We both sat in silence then. Although no words were spoken, it felt like we were still communicating. There was a bond between us, and even if we never met again, we would not be far from each other. I knew that Isaac and I would be friends forever. We touched hands and went our separate ways.

I headed back to Crooked River, and when I returned I found hardly any time had passed—only enough for me to have walked there and back. It was as though time spent with Isaac had been no time at all. I took out my crystal and gazed at it, wondering how someone as insignificant as I could have any power to make a difference.

Chapter 11

Going Home

It was Tuesday, the day before I was to leave the island. I prepared to head back to England and the rat race. Mary and I walked down to Cross Road to catch the bus for May Pen. As the bus sped off, music blaring, I took a last look at the passing scenery that had been my home for the last month. Part of me was sad I was leaving, but I would be glad to see the children again. My youngest daughter, Katie, had rang me every week telling me what was going on back home. Plus, my money would soon run out. I was ready to start back to work and get back to normal. That was, if anything could ever be normal again, after the experiences with Isaac, the crystal, and the dreams. I knew that tell anyone of what Isaac had told me would be to open myself up to ridicule, yet all these things that I had experienced could not go to waste. They needed to be told. But I had no idea how that could be done.

Through Crystal Clear Waters

When we reached May Pen, I purchased some gifts to take back home, mostly trinkets, mugs, and wall plaques with Jamaican scenes on them—and of course several bottles of white rum. We went to the fish market, where avenues of middle-aged women were selling all different kinds of fish. They were all sat with their skirts slapped between their legs. Next to their boxes of fish were a set of scales and a bucket of water to rinse their hands. The area was concrete, with a drainage channel running along the front of the stalls, separating the women from the customers. The smell of fish was pungent and fish scales were flying around as the women prepared them for the customers. The women called out to try to lure people to their stalls, a lot of them eating oranges as they sold. I wondered how they could eat the oranges while their hands were wet with the fish,. It couldn't be very appetising. I was glad to get out of the market and back into the fresh air.

After going for patties (a pastry with meat or fish filling) and a drink, we headed off back to catch the bus to Crooked River. We took some curried goat home to the men and brought some rum and raisin ice cream in a large tub for us all to dip in.

Later, while Mary was cooking the fish, I started making notes of all the things Isaac had told me, so as not to leave anything out when I reached home. Later, we

Going Home

tucked into a meal of snapper fish, cabbage, yam, and banana, afterwards sitting on the veranda for the last evening to chat the night away.

Wednesday morning came; I woke early to catch the last glimpse of the dawn on the island. I listened to the birds singing, cocks crowing, and donkeys braying, the first rays of sun appear over the mountain, and the mists rise up from the valleys. As I washed my face for the last time in the morning dew, I knew I was going to miss this Garden of Eden called Jamaica.

I would miss the hospitality shown to me by Mary and Bee, and the friendliness of everyone in this Crooked River community. The place captivated me, and I knew I would return one day. I had found an inner peace here, an escape from the rat race, and had got back in tune with myself. But most of all, I had found a new purpose to life. I had found what I thought I had lost. I decided to write more poems and get some articles published on a website, to try to get people to wake up to what humanity should be doing. I wanted to travel, learn, and make a difference.

As the music started coming from the houses and everyone started going about their daily life, I finished packing my suitcase, preparing things for the journey. Eli was travelling back to England with me and the car was to pick us up at midday. The flight to

Through Crystal Clear Waters

England was to leave the Norman Manley Airport in Kingston at 4:30 p.m., arriving in Gatwick at 7:30 a.m. Thursday.

With everything done and ready, there were still a couple of hours left to wait for the car. I sat out on the veranda eating some spice bun and cheese. All morning people had passed bidding me good-bye and wishing me a safe journey home. The children too, had waved and shouted 'bye. I saw a familiar form walking slowly, kicking stones with his bare feet, both hands in his pockets with his head hung down, coming up to the house. It was Kendrick. I had been hoping to see him before I went, as I was going to give him a few dollars. He reached the veranda and leaned on the wall. I gave him the money and we bid each other good-bye. As I looked at his face I could see he was fighting back a tear, and he again hung his head and shuffled off and sat on a bench across the road from the house. He sat there for about ten minutes. I watched him as he played with his fingers in a nervous way, occasionally wiping his eyes with the back of his hand, before taking one last look across at me on the veranda, then running off down the road. I felt a lump in my throat, and tears began to roll down my cheeks. What was to become of this young boy who did not want to go to school? What would the next ten years bring for Kendrick? I wished there was

Going Home

more I could do for this young boy, but maybe that chance would come if his dream of us meeting in the future came true. I felt like I was leaving my family behind. I had fallen in love with this island that had taught me so much.

The time came, and after saying our good-byes to Mary and Bee, we set off on the two-hour ride to Kingston. I was silent the whole time, just looking out of the window. Just past May Pen, on a series of bends, I looked for a place that had always caught my eye on that stretch of road. There was a small house on one side and on the other was a seat that looked like a throne, carved out of an old tree stump. Both were painted brightly in traditional Jamaican colours of green, yellow, red, and black. I had first seen them when I had visited nine years before and was surprised to see them there just the same on this trip. As we passed them, there was a young man sitting on the throne seat, and as I looked I saw it was Isaac. I turned to watch him as the car passed. He was waving with that familiar smile on his face. I watched as we drove on, until I couldn't see him anymore.

As we reached Kingston, the heavens opened and the rain poured down, ending the dry spell that had lasted just over a couple of weeks. There was so much rain that the electrics failed at the airport and the flight was delayed for forty-five minutes. It was too heavy for

Through Crystal Clear Waters

the plane to take off. I remembered what Bee had said to me the night before: "Chiane, Jamaica will cry the day you leave."

I sat waiting for the huge plane to take off, picking up speed until that familiar feeling of rising up into the sky. As I looked out of the window, I saw everything on the ground getting smaller and smaller. The plane circled round to take up its flight path, and I watched as the shape of the island disappeared into the distance.

Chapter 12

Reality

I was heading home. My thoughts turned to my children and grandchildren. I was the first person to hold my latest grandchild, a beautiful little boy called Darnell. When he was born eight months ago, he was placed into my hands by the midwife in the hospital. His father was a Jamaican from May Pen. My daughter Maria was bringing him up on her own, helped by her younger sister Katie and me. I thought that when Darnell was old enough, I would bring him to Jamaica, so he too could experience the island of his ancestors.

I opened up the bundle I had carefully packed into my hand luggage and gazed at the piece of crystal Isaac had given me. As I looked deep into it, my mind reflected on its beauty. This was such a precious piece; no amount of money could buy it.

Where had Isaac got this exquisite piece of crystal? Could it have been handed down to him from his ancestors? And what sort of information did it hold?

Through Crystal Clear Waters

Isaac had told me when he gave me the crystal that it was special, full of information, and that it would help me dream. I began to wish I had asked more questions about it. But I had the feeling I would find out the secret the crystal held all by myself. Whenever Isaac had told me anything, he always seemed to stop at the most interesting moment, leaving me to work out the answers for myself. They were parables or riddles, rather like my dreams as an adult.

The thought of working out everything made me despair of ever making sense of all the events that had taken place over the last month. Many a time I had become exasperated, trying to figure out my dreams, so much so that I often gave up, wishing I hadn't had the dream in the first place. But I could never ignore them, because later, all would be revealed. Then, I always looked back and saw the significance of the dreams and would mentally kick myself that I had not been able to work them out, wondering if I could have altered anything.

Most dreams never foretold of anything good. They were usually warnings of things that could go wrong. So I was often left thinking 'I could have stopped that happening'. But, I wondered, what good were dreams if all they were going to tell me were of things that would cause problems?

Reality

I remembered that not all my dreams had been experienced while I was sleeping. I could be wide awake, going about my everyday business, and have what was known as a vision. As I sat, gazing at the clouds, I reflected on such a vision I had had several years ago. It had been a usual hectic day. Hugh had caught a stomach bug and was off work sick. He was a diabetic, and although he was constantly throwing up in a bowl, I thought he was being a typical man, feeling sorry for himself. My two eldest girls, ages five and three-and-a-half, were fighting over a toy. Their dad needed constant attention, and to top it all, my washing machine had sprung a leak, flooding the kitchen floor. To say I was stressed was an understatement.

My friend Christine called round with her husband and two children as all this was going on. They brought with them a big red pedal car they had just bought for their eldest daughter's birthday. This led my eldest to follow me around the wet kitchen floor asking me if she could have a car, constantly asking, can I, Mum, please? My patience with her was running desperately thin.

As I stood at the kitchen sink washing the pots, I gazed out of the window. All of a sudden, the back garden transformed itself into the main front road, with an ambulance speeding by with its sirens blowing and lights flashing. I blinked and shook my head,

Through Crystal Clear Waters

but the vision was still there when I looked back out of the window. I stopped washing up and sat down in the kitchen, telling Christine what had just happened. I thought I was going mad, probably because I was having such a bad day. My friend put the kettle on and told me to relax, saying she would make me a cup of coffee, telling me I was just stressed. She gave me my coffee and took a cup of tea into the lounge for my husband. Suddenly, she ran back into the kitchen, telling me Hugh had collapsed and she could not wake him.

I rushed into the lounge to find him slumped on the settee. We could not rouse him at all. I quickly phoned the doctor, who arrived within fifteen minutes. The doctor informed me, that he was in a diabetic coma and promptly called for an ambulance. Ten minutes later the ambulance was arriving at the front of the house, with sirens blowing and lights flashing, just as I had seen in the vision. Forty minutes after looking out of the kitchen window, my husband was being whisked off to hospital in an ambulance. He had not taken his insulin since feeling unwell and had gone into a coma.

My friend was amazed by the series of event that had taken place, telling me she would never have believed it had she not witnessed it all. She kept saying the whole thing was "spooky," and that anything weird

Reality

I ever would tell her from now on, she would take seriously.

After about a week, my husband was back at work and everything was back to normal. Christine never let me forget that day and would tell the story to her friends for years to come. As for me, it was just something that always happened. It was not the first and it would not be the last.

I looked down at the piece of crystal in my hand and pondered what secret it held, where it would lead me to, and what sort of trouble was I going to get myself into now. I knew life would never be the same again since my meeting with Isaac. I placed the crystal back into my bag, closed my eyes, and drifted off to sleep.

It didn't seem long before the plane touched down in Gatwick. Sleep had made the journey go quickly, and as the plane thundered down the runway, I thought to myself, I am home.

Eli's daughter and grandson had come with the taxi to pick us up. On reaching Nottingham, they were dropped off first at Eli's home. Then the taxi took me home. Katie and Maria were there to welcome me back and I was surprised how much Darnell had grown since I had been away. He had just started to crawl. Over the next couple of days, my other children visited and collected their rum and gifts.

Through Crystal Clear Waters

The following week I signed a new contact with the technology dept at the college I worked for, and started back to work and the practicalities of life. For the next few months, I threw myself into it; we had started a new project of which I was the organiser, trying to get our adult Internet technology students into work experience placements. There were numerous people to see, paperwork to be designed and set in place, and endless funding plans and promotional work to undertake. This didn't leave many moments to reflect on my journey to paradise.

Several years passed with various projects completed, and I had just spent the last few months setting up the latest venture to take education into several large local workplaces. But when things were getting underway and everything was going to plan, the pace slowed down a little, I had more time to relax. My grandchildren had been arriving fast and furious, too. Katie had two girls, Courteney and Kady. Bridget had a daughter, Latayia, and a son, Kai. James had also had two girls, Jessica and Emily. Between work and family there didn't seem like a moment to spare. One evening, I poured myself a whisky and ran myself a nice warm bubble bath, planning to have an early night. I lit a few aromatic candles and lay back in the creamy bubbles, feeling I had earned my little luxury after all the hard work I had put in lately.

Reality

Then, in a sudden flash of inspiration, I remembered the crystal. I had been so busy, I had not even thought about it since placing the precious bundle into my jewellery box. With a sense of urgency, I jumped out of the bath, grabbed my robe, and took out the piece. As I unwrapped it and looked once again on its purity and beauty, I remembered Isaac had said it would help me dream, something I had not done since returning home and getting back to work. I carefully placed the crystal under my pillow and settled down to go to sleep.

That night, my dream began with me walking down a long, white-painted corridor. In the background I could vaguely make out some music playing, but it seemed far in the distance and I could not decipher the tune. There was not a soul in sight and the corridor seemed to go on forever. I continued to walk, seemingly getting nowhere. I must have been walking for ages when I stopped, turning around to see how far I had come. To my amazement, there was a solid white wall approximately two feet behind me. I thought, this could not be right, and panic struck in as I realised there was no going back.

I resigned myself to keep going forward, as I had no choice. All that was going through my mind was that I had to get out of there, so on I went, quickening my pace, hoping to come to the end of the corridor. A

Through Crystal Clear Waters

couple of times I stopped and glanced behind me, to see how much progress I had made. But each time I did, my heart sank, as that solid wall was still two feet behind me. I didn't seem to be getting anywhere at all. I could feel my heart beating faster. I was beginning to lose hope of ever finding a way out.

I sat down on the floor and viewed the corridor. The floor was grey marble, with the walls and ceiling brilliant white. It was about three feet wide by seven feet high. There were no doors, and just like that solid wall behind, the distance ahead never changed, either. The corridor was lit by a series of ceiling lights, just like the view from a hospital trolley, going down to the theatre for an operation. I felt nervous, as if that was exactly what I was doing. The only thing I could do was keep going. I noticed I could now recognise the tune that was playing. It was John Lennon, singing "Imagine." This had always been a favourite tune of mine and as I listened to the words, my spirits lifted. On and on I went as the song got louder and louder—just like the corridor, never seeming to end.

One last time I decided to look behind me. This time there was no solid wall but a white door with a red handle on the left-hand side. I breathed a sigh of relief; at last I could get out of here. I apprehensively put my hand on the door handle, not knowing what I would find behind it. I shut my eyes tightly and slowly

Reality

opened the door, which felt heavy and creaked as I pulled it towards me. I felt a blast of warm air on my face and opened my eyes.

To my surprise, I stood at the doorway of a plane, with the steps in place to go down to the tarmac. I started down, looking around as I did so. There were a number of planes' lined up on either side, but not one single person to be seen—no passengers, no airport workers, no one at all. The whole place was deserted, except for me. I walked through the checkout, through the main gate, and out into the open, there was still not a soul to be seen. The airport itself seemed familiar. It was right on the coast and as I looked out at the clear blue sea, rippling onto white sands dotted with coconut palms, I began to realise this was just like the airport at Montego Bay in Jamaica, although it seemed like a ghost town, with no people, no taxis—just me, all on my own.

I headed towards the beach to collect my thoughts. I kicked off my shoes and paddled in the clear sea along the coastline, with little waves refreshingly rippling over my feet. Although I didn't know where I was going or how to get back, and everywhere was so strangely deserted, I still felt calm and tranquil, as if nothing else mattered but the beauty of the beach. As I strolled a little further I could see the figure of an old man ahead of me, sitting facing the sea under the shade of a palm tree. I started up the beach towards him, shouting hello and waving.

The old man watched me as I approached him. He had long black hair tied behind him going all the way down his back, a goatee beard, and a thin moustache. Looking into his big, dark eyes, I saw they had all the brightness and sparkle of youth, and there was something about him very familiar. Then it came to me. "Izacal?" I asked as I stood before him.

"What took you so long? "

I asked what he meant, and he told me it had been years since he had spoken to me of my journey. Since I had returned home, I had forgotten everything. He had been waiting for what seemed like a lifetime for me.

I remarked jokingly that it must have been a lifetime, as he was a young man the last time I had spoken with him, and now he looked about seventy. Quite sternly he told me that age was just like time, irrelevant, and was not worth joking about.

I felt quite shocked at his rebuke and defended myself by saying that if time was irrelevant, why was he asking me what took me so long?

Izacal started laughing and said, "Calm down. Your Western urgency has made you tense again. Time is more irrelevant to me than it is for you; I can't wait another thirty years to tell you what to do to find yourself, because for you that would be too late!" He patted the sand next to him, indicating for me to sit down. As we sat, he explained how he had taken me on my journey, led me to meet Isaac, and had thought I would return home with the inspiration to do what I had been born to do. He thought I had found myself, but ever since I had returned home I had been in danger of getting lost again. Had I forgotten the conversations with him and Isaac? If not, what did I intend to do?

I felt ashamed and hung my head. All the experiences on my journey, and I had just gone back to the hustle and bustle of everyday life, forgetting who I was and what I had intended to do.

"Don't worry," Izacal said as he lifted my face to look him in his eyes. "The daughters take a little longer, but you'll get there."

We smiled at each other. Izacal told me he had to go but that I would see him again, as he was not going to give up on me. He suggested I take a little nap under the palm tree before I went home, and bid me good-bye. I watched him walk away, lay back and closed my eyes.

The next thing I knew, I was waking up in my bed with that strange humming sound in my ears. I sat

Through Crystal Clear Waters

up and took the crystal from under my pillow; it was glowing. As I looked at the crystal, remembering my dream, the humming faded and it was no longer glowing. I vowed to myself I would never forget again and placed the crystal under my pillow, where it would stay—ensuring a lot more dreamtime adventures.

I drifted back to sleep, but I was awoken abruptly by the telephone ringing. I rushed downstairs and within a few moments, realised this phone call was about to embark me on my next journey of discovery.

Chapter 13

Taking a chance

It was 4:20 a.m. when the phone rang. Running down the stairs, I expected it to be one of the children with a problem and so was feeling a bit worried as I picked it up.

"Hey Chiane, what are you up to?" a voice greeted me.

"Dusty! Do you know what time it is?" He told me it was mid-evening over in Texas, but what he had to tell me was too important to wait. He knew I would understand.

I first met Dusty Jack many years ago on a field trip to Stonehenge. We had become instant friends, the kind that you think you have known for years, ten minutes after meeting them. There was a special connection, ever since I told him at breakfast at the guest house we were staying at, that I had dreamt he found his wallet next to one of the stones at the site. On checking his pockets, he realised he had lost it,

Through Crystal Clear Waters

so we both set off, and sure enough found it exactly where my dream said it would be. We had kept in constant contact over the Internet ever since, if he got himself into a tricky situation, which happened quite often, he always rang me for advice, and I had got him out of a few scrapes over the years. He accepted me for who I was, without question or doubt, saying my eccentric character made life much more interesting and said we both a right pair of crazy's. I had been to visit him in Texas, and we had spent many hours chatting about ancient civilisations, such as the Mayans, Aztecs and Inca. Understanding the ancients was one of my pet subjects, and we had taken quite a few trips to the sites whilst I was there. Dusty was an archaeologist who did a lot of digs to discover these ancient cities—hence his nickname. Now, the tone in his voice told me he was excited.

"Chi, you will really want to hear this. One of my colleagues is on a dig in Chichen Itza; they are uncovering more tunnels under and around the Pyramid of Kukulcan. He rang me about an hour ago saying he had found something and had taken it back to his campsite to decipher what it said. He reckons it told of the whereabouts, under the temple, of a fifth and sixth Mayan calendar. He claims he will reach where it is supposed to be located in about one month."

Taking a chance

"Oh my gosh," I replied. "Just that information alone will be of value, especially as we are approaching two thousand twelve. Was it on stone or parchment?"

"He didn't specify, but what he did say was that it gave a warning about who should gain knowledge of the new cycles, and that some would kill for that information. Many world powers would not want this information made public, and so the calendar is not stored in its usual format."

I felt a tingle going down my spine. "So Dusty, this has an element of 'handle with care,' don't you think?"

"Definitely, Chi, but I want you with me on this one. Can you be ready in the next two weeks?"

I was silent for a few minutes; pondering my work situation, family, mortgage—but also remembering the dream I had that night and my pledge to myself to undertake another adventure.

"Chi–are you still there?" Dusty's voice roused me.

"Yeah, Dusty, give me some time to figure things out, and I will get back to you."

His voice changed to imply certain urgency. "Make it quick, Chi. We can't afford to hang around on this one. Tell me when and I will book your flight."

Through Crystal Clear Waters

I needed time to think, so I told Dusty I would definitely ring him back tomorrow evening. I put the phone down and sat back, lit up a cigarette, and tried to put some sense into what I could be about to undertake.

Naturally, I was inspired to take that gigantic leap into the unknown. I knew everyone would think I had gone completely bonkers, as it meant risking my job, and my financial situation wasn't great. I wondered how long I would be away, and what would we do with this artefact if we found it. What dangers would be involved? My mind reflected on what Myrtle had said before we parted in Jamaica, her warning about not trusting everyone on my next trip abroad. There was no way I could sleep, so after about an hour of pacing around, puzzling out the ifs and buts, I finally came to my conclusion: "What the hell, I'm going."

All my life I had had dreams, studied ancient cultures, and planned to travel to discover more. I had thought I had lost myself when life had left no time for me to pursue them. I had always thought there was something missing.

But the journey I had taken a few years ago had been an awakening. After Izacal's preachings and the time spent with Isaac in Jamaica, the future seemed without limits. I would be a fool not to go.

Taking a chance

I knew that if I remained trapped in my run-of-the-mill life of job, bills, and mortgage, I would never be fulfilled. I began to lay out a plan of action.

I went to work the next day, setting all the paperwork into place to take my current project through to its conclusion. I ran everything through with my replacement organiser, passed on contacts, and gave two weeks' notice, deciding to use that time to direct everyone on what needed to be done. I also contacted an estate agent, instructing him to put my house on the market. By the time I got home that evening, the "for sale" board was up. I had done it. There was no turning back now. I was free.

I rang Dusty around 10:00 p.m. to confirm I would be taking him up on his offer to join him, which was received much to his delight. He told me he would e-mail my flight details and would meet me in Houston in a fortnight's time, saying he thought I had made the right decision.

I knew that only Dusty would see the sense in all this and sure enough, for the rest of that week, my children tried to dissuade me from making what they thought to be a terrible mistake. They threw things at me like:

"Have you gone completely mad?"

Through Crystal Clear Waters

"What about us?"

"You're giving up everything to do something absolutely crazy!"

But they knew what I was like, which meant all they were saying was falling on deaf ears. Once I made up my mind about something, no one could persuade me otherwise.

The next Friday I left work for the last time. I had secured a prospective buyer for the house and packed up my possessions in containers to be stored with the children. I had placed Maria and Katie in charge of managing my affairs, signing papers to give them power of attorney to complete the house sale whilst I was away. My daughters seemed a little more at ease with the fact that they would have control over my finances, ensuring them when Ii returned to England, I would not have spent the majority of the money from the house on what they considered to be a reckless and stupid whim. Having a nest egg to come back to put their minds at rest, although they gave me a list of instructions of what to do—namely, avoid alligators, snakes, spiders, and any other wild animals, as well as terrorists or other "not very nice people."

Two weeks after Dusty's phone call, I was all packed and my children were once again seeing me off. This good-bye was a lot more emotional. With no return ticket, I did not know when I would be back. I promised them that I would be coming home and would keep in contact with them by phone. So with good-byes said, I was once again on my way to the airport. I felt energised. I was about to realize the ambitions of adventure I had as a young girl.

Chapter 14

Into the Unknown

I left Birmingham International airport, flying Continental, heading for Newark in the States, where I would take a connecting flight to Houston. It was long, but time passed quickly as I refreshed my mind, thumbing through all my Mayan research and bringing myself up to date on the Mayan calendar—which ended on 1 December 2012. Some from the Western world believed that the Mayans had foretold that the world would end on that date. But I had spoken to Mayan elders a few years ago when visiting Mexico with Dusty and had asked them about their calendar and the predictions. The elders had told me it was just the end of the fourth cycle and that their ancestors had never said there would not be another cycle. Although they may have predicted the end of the world and how it might happen, they had never put a date on the event.

I knew that 21 December was the start of the winter solstice every year and that the Age of Aquarius was set to begin on that date in 2012, so the idea of a new cycle made perfect sense to me. I was eager that it would be Dusty and I that would be the first ones to find the artefact. To uncover the revelations it might hold made me very excited. By the energy in his voice when we spoke on the phone, I knew that Dusty had already come to the same conclusion. I was sure that Izacal would be proud of me and was convinced he would dream me my next steps.

Soon I was hitting the runway at Houston, collecting my baggage, and heading out. I could see Dusty frantically waving at me as I headed towards him. We hugged and gave each other a knowing smile at what we were about to undertake as we left on the long drive to his house.

Once on the road, Dusty asked me if I had told anyone about the find and what we were planning to do. I told him I hadn't gone into detail, only telling folks we were going on an archaeological dig together. I had presumed that if it got out exactly what we were looking for, we might be faced with a crowd of people chasing after the same thing. I also told him that that I had had a hell of a job convincing my kids of the rationality of what I was doing, without going into specifics.

Into the Unknown

"Good, good, good," replied Dusty in his usual manner. "Because my friend's life might be at risk should this get out."

I was shocked. "What do you mean *at risk?* In what way?" And, "are we at risk?" Dusty looked across at me grinning, saying he didn't have the answers. His friend had rung him a week ago expressing these concerns, but he would not elaborate over the phone. He had only stressed we should get there as soon as possible, when he would explain everything, and that we needed to keep it quiet until then. Dusty said he had noticed deep anxiety in his friend's voice that he had never heard before.

We drove the rest of the way to Dusty's house in silence. I was trying to absorb what he had just told me, asking myself what on earth I had got myself into now. I remembered my children's cautionary warnings. Maybe I should have listened to them. Panic began to set in. But then, I reasoned, venturing into the unknown always held some risks. This artefact was probably just a piece of stone or something. All we were going to do was find it and give it to some museum. Where was the danger in that? I came to the conclusion that Dusty was exaggerating the dangers and that Ben was just worried that someone else might beat him to discovering this thing. I calmed myself down.

Through Crystal Clear Waters

We reached Dusty's home. I took my suitcase up to my room, and then we sat down, lit up a cigarette, and poured a drink—whisky for me and large dark rum for Dusty.

"Are you sure you are up for this, Chi?" Dusty asked as he sat back with his rum.

"Of course," I said. "I have given up everything for this artefact. In for a penny, in for a pound. I'm not going to give up now!"

Dusty smiled. "I knew I could rely on you. We leave for Mexico tomorrow. I have a hire car waiting at Cancun, where we will drive to a little town called Pisté, a few miles from Chichen Itza, to meet up with Ben."

We had a bit of a catch-up. I told him all about my trip to Jamaica, of meeting up with Isaac, and the mysteries he had shown me. Dusty listened with great interest, and as I expected, put in his ideas as to what it all meant. Then he suggested we should both get some rest. We were to spend a night chilling in Cancun, so we would be ready for the journey ahead. There would be no "mod cons" at the campsite, he said.

We bid each other good-night and retired to bed. I took my piece of crystal out of my bag and placed it under my pillow. I lay down thinking that if ever I needed a spirit guide, now was the time. Izacal had better give me a dream tonight to tell me what the hell is going on. With that thought, I gently drifted to sleep.

Waking the next morning, I felt disappointed at not having a dream to instruct me on the quest I was about to take, but reassured myself Izacal would speak to me soon. I went downstairs to make a coffee and found a note from Dusty on the fridge, saying he had gone to get some provisions for our trip. Taking my coffee, I sat out on the deck, taking in the view across the lake. It was a beautiful morning, hardly any clouds, with the temperature already in the mid-seventies. I watched as eagles soared overhead and herons landed at the lake's edge. This was such a tranquil place, with not another soul in sight, apart from an occasional speedboat across the other side of the lake. I could totally understand why Dusty had decided to locate here. It was so relaxing. After drinking my coffee, I decided to take a swim in the pool.

Dusty returned around midday. We had something to eat while discussing our plans and speculating about what the next cycle of the Mayan calendar might say. We packed our backpacks into the Jeep and set off to the Houston airport to fly to Cancun. We discussed many things, but neither of us spoke of the dangers that might lie ahead. Dusty had booked us into one of the best hotels for the night, saying he figured we deserved a bit of luxury before going to the site. After getting the keys to our rooms and taking a shower to refresh from all the travelling, we met up in the lobby and headed off for a night in Cancun town centre. After having a lovely meal in the Hacienda da Morte, being entertained by the mariachi band, we set off for the bars.

In the morning I awoke early and took a walk along the Caribbean Sea coast, outside the hotel. The crystal-clear blue sea was as pure as any spring water, and the sand was bleached white. Walking back along the beach, I saw Dusty walking towards me. "Are you ready?" he asked. I confirmed my eagerness. We got our things, handed in the keys, and had a margarita in the hotel bar before setting off.

The further we drove outside Cancun, the more poverty was apparent. I thought, we were heading to a place where an ancient civilisation had such a great empire, with giant pyramids and temples. Yet here, thousands of years later, people live in such poverty and hunger. What on Earth had gone wrong? Why could not the opulent West, with all our technologies and profits, make sure all the people of the world had a decent standard of living? Many of the houses we saw had only two rooms, made of bare concrete block, not even painted. One was used for cooking and washing, the other for living. The only furniture visible was a small table with a couple of chairs—not even a bed. Dusty told me that at night they would just hook up hammocks to sleep. I was saddened and disgusted by what I was seeing, even a bit ashamed by my own comfy lifestyle.

"That's the way things are, kid," said Dusty. I sighed. "You should see what happens on a Sunday. They all dress up in their Sunday best clothes to attend church. The people here are very religious. Church is a very important part of their lives. After the service, they all gather in the town centre, which is usually just outside the church, for an evening of music and food. They have a good community spirit, especially after the Sunday service. Everything revolves around that."

I responded that I still felt sad they had to live in such poverty and that having a Sunday knees-up did not compensate for their day-to-day hardships.

Along the road there were quite a few shrines, made out of rocks and beautifully decorated. Dusty said they were erected when somebody had been killed on the road. I was also intrigued as to why, where there were no houses, there were strange objects hanging from the thick jungle of trees on either side of the road—sometimes an old tyre or a crate, or just pieces of rag, seemingly at regular intervals. Dusty told me they indicated the location of dwellings deep within the bush. I thought, oh my God, things just got worse. What a difference from the luxurious hotel, with its views of the Caribbean Sea that we had left, just a few hours ago.

We travelled on and soon reached Pisté, a small town located about an hour west of Valladolid, in the middle of the state of Yucatan. Pisté's only industry came from the fact that it is about a mile from the ruins of Chichen Itza, the most awe-inspiring of the Mayan ruins. The stores were full of Itza trinkets—tribal masks, hand-carved statues, miniature pyramids, crystal skulls, and other pieces of craftwork out of woven or carved bamboo or obsidian. The gift shops only took up a small part of the town and locals could often be seen in the evening, sitting on chairs outside their homes in the street, chatting or watching a shared television. There were also a lot of food vendors and bars. So we parked the car outside a bar near the centre of the town, got a beer, and sat waiting at a table on the veranda for Ben to arrive.

About twenty minutes later, a shabby, unshaven, middle-aged Englishman, quite short in stature, came and sat down at our table. He and Dusty hugged each other and I was introduced to Ben, who cautiously shook my hand. I noticed he seemed very nervous. He kept looking over his shoulder, as if he expected someone to be following him. There was fear in his eyes as he requested we drink up and go with him to the campsite, where we could talk.

We set off in Ben's car, deeper into the jungle, until we reached the place where he had set up camp, just on the outskirts of Chichen Itza. He poured us a coffee from a pot he had suspended by a stick, kept warm over an open fire. He went into his tent and came out, starting to unwrap something from an old cloth—a roll of parchment. He sat down and began to tell us what he had deciphered.

Ben seemed both excited and agitated as he told us what he had deciphered, periodically looking around as if he expected to find someone listening in. Deep under the great pyramid of Kukulcan, he said, there was an alcove along the tunnel they were excavating, holding a fifth- and sixth-cycle calendar—not in stone or on parchment, but with its information infused into a piece of crystal. He began with how, after finding the parchment hidden in a clay pot, he had rolled the end of the parchment down and read the symbols relating to the fifth and sixth calendar and the object containing their location. Realising its importance, he had quickly rolled it back up and concealed it inside his shirt, planning to read it when he was alone.

He knew his team was now about three days away from reaching that location. As he was the only official archaeologist on that part of the dig, he had arranged for us to accompany him. He also planned to send the local helpers off for a few days' break. He was able to justify that to his sponsors, since there was a religious festival that weekend that was extremely important to the locals. That meant only the three of us would be at the site. No one else knew anything about his first find.

Ben told us of how, when the light began to fail, the local helpers had gone home. Ben had gone straight back to his campsite, poured a coffee, went inside his tent, and zipped up. He had unrolled the parchment and began to read. Dusty and I were mesmerised by the story he now told us of why the Mayans had used crystal to store the information of the calendar, and why they felt the need to hide it.

Chapter 15

The Secret

The story began with how the Mayans had been undergoing great changes around 320 BC. The Itza community was part of the great expansion of the Mayans, founding many ceremonial centres. The Itza also founded Chichen Itza in the Yucatan. Over a period of approximately fifty years, the Mayans had founded around thirty-five centres, with populations of mostly farmers. Around 830 BC many of the centres were abandoned, mainly through lack of guidance. They evacuated from areas around Guatemala to the Yucatan, repopulating Chichen Itza.

The Xiŭe were already established in the Yucatan at the time. They were an Uto-Aztec family and had dwelled there several centuries before the Mayans had arrived. Xiŭe were a warrior tribe and were more interested in weapons and making war, especially on this sudden influx of peace-loving Mayans.

In 940 BC the Toltecs arrived in the Yucatan. Their leader united with the Mayans to force the Xiue from

Through Crystal Clear Waters

Uxmal, and they fled, finding shelter in Tihoo. The Toltecs had been guided by their king, Quetzalcoatl, from the Mexico Valley to the Yucatan. When the Toltec king died, he was divinized as a god by both the Toltecs and the Mayans. They named him Kukulcan. The main pyramid in Chichen Itza is in honour of Kukulcan.

The Mayan men could not marry a girl from their own town. One young man took a wife from the Inca people, who originated in Peru, and went to live with her family. One day, the young man returned to Chichen Itza to warn them about a prediction of the high priests of the Inca, begging a meeting of the priests from both civilisations. The priests held the meeting, which took several days. The Inca told the Mayans they would be invaded by people from another landmass and must protect their history and scripts, because these people would steal their heritage. They also taught the Mayan priests how to store their information into pieces of crystal, telling them to hide the crystals where no one could find them, so as to protect their ancestry. They told them that at some point in the future when it was safe, the crystals would be found, and along with other pieces would be taken to a sacred place for the truth to be declared in a time of need.

The high priests returned to Chichen Itza, locked themselves away in the temple, and set about storing information into a piece of crystal the Inca had given

The Secret

them. The whole of the fifth cycle and the beginnings of a sixth was input, along with the complete set of the first three to the present fourth cycle. This took almost a year to complete, and then they hid it in a clay pot deep under the temple of Kukulcan, in a small chamber at the end of a long winding passage. They blocked parts of the passage as they returned to the surface.

Over the years there were quite a few wars between the Itzas, Toltecs, Xiue, and Uxmal, but nothing compared to the event that would destroy this glorious civilisation. In AD 1527, a Spaniard by the name of Francisco de Montejo conquered several Mayan cities. Chichen Itza defended itself well, but eventually fell at the hands of Montejo's son around four years later. By 1548, the whole of the Yucatan was controlled by the Spanish conquest.

We listened in amazement to all Ben told us, commenting on how much interest this would have to the media. We tried to persuade Ben to declare his find.

Ben was indignant. "You don't understand–there is more."

Shocked by his attitude, we asked him to explain. He told us there was a cautionary footnote on the scroll, telling of events that could prevent the crystal from reaching the right hands. There would be evil people who hand out, "bad seeds that dream man's mind."

Wanting power and riches, these people would kill anyone who had or knew the hidden information. They knew the knowledge would destroy their empire and awaken mankind to a better way, and would stop all the evil in the world.

The ancients had known and practised this information, but it was taken by the conquistadors and corrupted. Its properties were poisoned to spur man's mind to evil instead of good. But the evil ones knew there was hidden information and did not want it found. They themselves did not know where it was hidden and had been searching for centuries.

"Ben, you ain't scared of old wives' tales, are you?" Dusty retorted. "Something like this would not have put you off in the old days."

Ben grabbed Dusty by the shoulders and shook him, saying, "Don't you get it? Seeds that dream a man's mind—its drugs, Dusty, drugs! And the empire affected by losing power and riches are the drug cartels. If this gets out, our lives are at risk!"

"Okay, okay, I get it," said Dusty, freeing himself from Ben's grip. Realising the enormity of all this, I angrily asked Ben, "If you knew all this, why didn't you destroy the parchment? And why did you involve us?"

Ben sat back with his head in his hands. "I have been an archaeologist all my life, so my conscience will not allow me to destroy something like this. The truth cannot be destroyed. I have to get that crystal, along with the parchment, into the right hands, whoever that may be. I couldn't do it on my own, so I called Dusty. He has the courage of a lion and a better knowledge of cultures and their beliefs than I do. I didn't know he was going to bring you along."

"Don't look at me like that, Chi," said Dusty, taking a pack of beers out his backpack. "I will take you back to Pisté in the morning if you want. I wasn't aware all this would happen when I asked you to come with me."

We opened a can of beer each and sat in silence drinking for a few minutes, before Dusty asked me what I wanted to do. I was thinking of all I had given up, and what Izacal had said in that dream before Dusty's phone call. I had to see this through now, no matter what the consequences.

"Sleep on it, Chi," said Dusty. "Tell me what you are going to do in the morning."

But I didn't need to think anything over. It was crystal-clear that this was my destiny. "Don't need to, Dusty," I replied. "Nothing's gonna stop me now."

"Good, good, good," he replied, in his usual jovial manner.

Chapter 16

Destiny

Daybreak came. After consuming our usual caffeine fix and a cigarette, the three of us headed into the dig site around the pyramid of Kukulcan. Several local helpers were already busy cleaning off artefacts, so while Ben and Dusty went down the tunnel passages that were being excavated, I set about helping, or rather dusting off artefacts using a small paintbrush. I carefully cleaned bits of pottery, carved bone and shell pieces, and many stone glyphs, logging all the finds and placing them in labelled containers. I felt very privileged to be handling these pieces, admiring the artwork carved or engraved over three thousand years ago. It was as if I was actually there, and the experience gave me tremendous satisfaction.

I continued to do this work until Friday, when Ben sent all the local helpers home to prepare for the religious ceremony that weekend, telling them to enjoy themselves and that he would see them next

Through Crystal Clear Waters

week. When everyone had left, Dusty beckoned me to come with them down the excavated passage under the great pyramid. It was cold, damp, and had a musty smell as we made our way down the stone steps to the long, winding passage they had been working on for the past few months. The passage was only about thirty inches wide and approximately five feet high, with the ceiling made of huge stone slabs. Dusty had to stoop as he made his way along; Ben, not much taller than I, bent his knees as he progressed. I, however, was the perfect height. Every so often, we had to scramble over rubble from roughly made walls that had been erected to block the passage along the way. Eventually we reached the end, where there was yet another wall, but much more care had been taken in its construction. On the centre stone was carved a jaguar, and by Ben's demeanour I knew we had reached the place indicated on the parchment.

Ben looked like a child unwrapping a Christmas present as the two men set about chiselling away at the stones in one corner of the wall. Twenty minutes later they had freed the first stone and laid it carefully on the ground. Dusty told me to light a candle to the gap to check for any gasses. When it was okay, he urged me to take a look inside the chamber.

"Can you see anything, Chi?" asked Dusty eagerly.

"Not with a candle. Pass me the flashlight," I answered. As my eyes became accustomed to the narrow band of light, I saw many artefacts neatly stacked around the chamber. I could detect the walls were decorated with carvings and hieroglyphs. The back wall seemed to be painted with scenes in bright colours of red, orange, and creamy white.

Ben asked, "Can you see a tomb?"

I eagerly scanned around the opening before answering, "No, it just looks like a cache of stuff."

Ben started grumbling to himself, but Dusty just encouraged him to take some more stones out of the wall so we could climb through into the chamber and explore with better light. This they did while I held the torch for them to see, and about forty minutes later, glistening with beads of sweat, they had made a big enough gap for us to crawl through.

I went through first, closely followed by Ben, then Dusty. As we shone our flashlights around, we could see the true beauty of the chamber. On the wall at the back there was a large painting of Kinich Ahau, the Mayan sun god, and a scene of two men playing the ballgame put on before a ceremony and that regularly resulted in human sacrifice, usually by beheading. There were also many very accurate drawings of plants and farming scenes. Ben seemed more interested in the glyphs on the side wall, trying to decipher and write things down on his notepad, while Dusty started going through the many artefacts spread around the chamber.

There was an abundance of pottery along with obsidian carvings, masks, and blades. Dusty pointed out a short pot, full of sharp obsidian spike-like tools, which he explained were used for bloodletting ceremonies. This was when the priests pierced their tongues or sliced their skin, but more commonly pierced their penis, collecting the blood to offer to the gods, before entering a trancelike state to communicate with their ancestors. The idea of this practice sent a shudder down my back as I thought how painful it must have been.

Ben called for Dusty to take a look at what he had found on the side wall. He didn't seem too bothered about the artefacts, which I found quite odd. He just kept moaning that there was no sign of the crystal. The two of them got busy deciphering the stone glyphs that surrounded a circular, calendar-like stone that stood out from the wall. I went over to take a closer look. It had dots and dashes on it, but no other details, which had led the boys to dismiss it as insignificant.

I noticed the centre of this stone was separate from the calendar-like circle around it. I took hold of the round bit and found I could turn it like a wheel on a spindle.

"What are you doing?" shouted Ben, angry and agitated. He made me jump, and I spun round, leaning back on the wall beside the calendar-like wheel. With a *whoosh*, a large portion of the wall moved backwards, making me fall flat on my backside on the floor of yet another passage.

"Oh my lord!" squealed Ben in excitement, "You've found a secret passage." And for the first time since we met, a smile came across his face.

"Yeah," said Dusty. "We were so busy working out these glyphs, we missed the obvious. Well done, Chi!" He helped me back up on my feet, amused by my fall.

We followed this passage for what seemed like an eternity. Ben reckoned we were outside the pyramid, still underground, and worked out that we were heading in the direction of the largest *cenote*, or large natural waterhole, on the site. It, again, had been very important in ceremonies. This was a well-designed passage narrow and strongly built, with large wooden lintels supporting the ceiling blocks. I wondered if it would lead us directly into the water of the cenote but rationalised that the tunnel would be flooded if that were the case. We followed the path until we reached a rough opening at the end of the passage, leading into an intricate maze of underground caves, not much taller but much wider than the tunnel.

Ben said we should follow the cave that had a sort of stream running through it, so off we went, deeper and deeper into the cave. It was nerve-wracking, as big black spiders kept dropping from massive cobwebs at the top of the low-roofed cave. Dusty laughed as I acted paranoid, knocking them off myself, making noises of disgust. As we paddled along the stream, it began getting deeper, more like a small river.

Just as we viewed what seemed like an end wall, *splash!* All three of us ended up in a sudden deep expanse of water that spanned the width of the cave, rather like an underground cenote, but much smaller. After splashing around in an attempt to get our bearings, Dusty dove down to see how deep it was while Ben and I swam to the end wall, floating around and shining our flashlights, looking around the cave. Dusty popped up, saying he had found a hole in the rocks and was going to swim through it to investigate.

"No Dusty!" I said. "It's much too dangerous."

But he ignored my warning. "Pull yourself together, Chi. I know my limitations. It would take more than that to finish off an old sea dog like me. If I don't get to the other side, I will turn back before I run out of air." And with that, down he went. He had spent his early years as a submariner for the British Navy, so I knew he was made of stern stuff.

That left me and Ben floating around. He seemed more amenable than he had when we first met, and we tried to make conversation. But I was more worried about Dusty, since several minutes had passed. Ben tried to reassure me he would be okay, but after around ten minutes, I told Ben to go down and check that nothing had happened to him. I worried that he could be snagged on something. Ben was just about to dive down when up popped Dusty. He had found another larger cave through the rocks, so after expressing my relief and concern, we all three took a deep breath and followed him through the hole in the rock.

We emerged into a wide cavern and found a way to clamber up out of the water onto a ledge, shining our flashlights. On exploring the ledge we came across a cradle like dip in the rock, which contained a skeleton. Judging by the obsidian neckpieces and wristbands, it appeared to be the bones of a high priest. There were also a number of jade beads, which probably would have adorned his robes. But much to Ben's disgust, there was no sign of the crystal. We persuaded Ben to return to the camp, telling him the cache back in the chamber was well worth the effort and that he should declare his find. Ben begrudgingly agreed to go back after searching every nook and cranny in the cave, moaning that the parchment had said the crystal was in a pot in the chamber. He was not a happy chappie.

We set off back underwater to the first cave, climbing out of the deep pool and along the stream, back underground to the chamber. Ben was getting more and more frustrated, grumbling and swearing as we went back, acting like a child who had just dropped his ice cream.

On reaching the chamber, Ben would not leave. He stayed checking the glyphs and searching every pot scattered around the chamber, stomping about, throwing pots around, and swearing profoundly. Dusty and I left him to it and returned to the campsite.

On the way back, Dusty told me of his concerns about Ben, saying something was not quite right. Ben was acting out of character, obsessed with finding the crystal, and not even bothered about the find under the pyramid. He spoke of his time alone with Ben prior to reaching the chamber, of how he had asked him where along the passage he had found the parchment. But Ben could not tell him, saying he had forgotten the exact location, Dusty said he had checked the whole passage on his way in and out and had found no such alcove that could have concealed the parchment. He had also asked Ben who had sponsored the dig and who was paying him, and again Ben had been elusive, becoming angry with Dusty. Why all the questions? He had asked.

Dusty could see no reason why Ben's sponsors had to be a secret, or why an archaeologist would "forget" where he had found an important parchment, showing no interest in the cache. He could, however, understand the need to keep the existence of the parchment secret, at least until finding the crystal. Just not the edgy fear for his life Ben seemed to have.

I, too, expressed my disappointment at not finding the crystal. It would have had much more cultural interest than any of the artefacts. But still, I had enjoyed the whole experience.

Dusty was not his usual jovial self. "See what you think when Ben comes back. I don't trust him. Something is wrong in all of this."

We made some coffee and sat smoking and chatting about the wall painting and artefacts till Ben returned. Dusk was setting in when Ben came back to the camp, and he was in a foul mood, cussing and pacing up and down, making statements like, "That's it, my life is over!" and, "How can I justify not finding the crystal?" Dusty and I looked at each other: Justify to whom? Even Dusty couldn't calm him down.

Ben agreed to let us take the car back to Pisté, saying we could stay at a room he had in the town. So Dusty and I left, while Ben remained at the campsite, still stomping around like a madman.

I was glad when we reached the room to get cleaned up and change my clothes. We sat down to discuss Ben's behaviour. "I can see what you mean; his attitude does not make any sense," I said, telling Dusty that I did not like the guy much. He seemed very self-centred and extremely paranoid. I enquired how he and Ben had become friends in the first place.

He told me they had met many years ago when they were young, serving on submarines in the Navy. Ben had been a sonar technologist, working out sounds. Doing that job had got him interested in deciphering hieroglyphs and ancient scripts. Since Dusty had been in the stores as a stock controller, they had been basically just drinking buddies. But their shared interest in archaeology had seen them meet up again much later in their chosen profession, and they had kept in touch. He told me Ben had not always been such a misery. But there had been a long time after their second dig together in which he had not heard from Ben, and the talk going around was that he had got into drugs. Dusty thought that maybe drugs had something to do with his moods, although they didn't account for his behaviour surrounding this dig. We spent the rest of the evening chatting away, wondering what our next move would be.

Chapter 17

Kidnapped

The next morning we drove back to the campsite, but there was no sign of Ben or his tent. Everything was gone.

"Now what do we do?" I said to Dusty. "The crazy old fool has taken off!"

Dusty answered in a sombre tone. "It's not like Ben to just 'take off.' Something's wrong, I tell you. We have his car, so where would he go? He didn't come back to the room. I'll try ringing his cell phone." Ben's phone rang, but no answer. "He might have it on silent. Let's go take a look around the site. Maybe he's set up camp in another location," said Dusty.

"More like he has no further use for us," I retorted.

We searched all over the ruins at Chichen and around the outskirts, calling out his name, but no luck. We even checked to see if he had gone back to the cache under the main pyramid, but nothing had been touched, apart from all the broken pots Ben had frantically gone through the day before. Dusty remarked that no archaeologist would have such disregard for such precious items by chucking them around and breaking them. He decided we should go back to Pisté, as Ben would probably turn up there sooner or later, suggesting we could go watch the religious ceremony and get something to eat. But I knew he was only trying to ease the situation. Dusty had always had a devil-may-care attitude to life—always smiling, nothing ever getting him down. But his face told me a different story right now, as concern was written all over it.

We stood on a corner of the main street outside a restaurant, to watch the route the procession was taking to the market square in front of the church. But I could see Dusty was not paying any attention. He was looking for Ben amongst the crowds, constantly watching the road leading to the ruins to see if he could catch sight of him returning. We had something to eat, sitting at one of the tables outside on the pavement in front of the restaurant, so Dusty could continue his surveillance. Then, after picking up some beer, we returned to the room. We sat chatting about these latest mysterious events and what our options were, until suddenly the door opened. We both looked round, expecting to see Ben.

A small, pretty Mexican woman in her late twenties came in, introducing herself as Blanca. She told us she was Ben's girlfriend and then burst into tears. We told her to sit down, made her a coffee, and tried to calm her, waiting to hear what she had to say. After she had taken a few sips of coffee, continuously thanking us, Dusty asked her if she knew where Ben was. We were amazed by what she told us.

"Mr Dusty, Miss Chiane, I am very worried! Ben rang me past midnight Friday night, telling me to get something for him as he had to go into hiding. He told me to bring his passport and some papers he kept in a box at my house, along with all the money he had hidden in there."

Dusty chipped in, "Hidden from whom? What is he frightened of?"

Blanca started crying again, telling us, "I did as he said and went to the campsite about 2:00 a.m., but there was no sign of him. I got frightened and came straight back. I have not heard from him since!"

Dusty started getting agitated, telling Blanca she still hadn't told us anything, and why the cloak and dagger stuff? I told Dusty to go easy on the girl and to just let her explain.

"Okay, okay," he said. "Tell us what happened, from the beginning."

Blanca continued, "Yes Mr Dusty, I try!"

Through Crystal Clear Waters

It seemed she had first met Ben over a year ago, when he came out with a whole team of archaeologists to a previous dig at the site, and they had begun a relationship. He had returned on his own a few months ago to continue alone with the dig and paid several local men to help him.

"Ben had a lot of money," she continued. "I mean much, much money. He was being paid by the Tercer Ojo, a group from the major drug cartels, which undertake investigation work for them. They had given him a parchment they had in their possession for many years. On hearing about the previous dig, they had contacted Ben, paying him thousands of dollars to return and find something the parchment had spoken about. Ben was happy he was rich and got on with the task. Friday night he told me he hadn't found what they wanted. When he rang them to tell them, they didn't believe him and threatened his life. That's why he was going into hiding. But I think they must have got him, Mr Dusty! Please help!"

Blanca then gave Dusty a bag that must have contained thousands of dollars—enough to buy a big house and a prestigious car outright, and still more after that.

Dusty started to pace up and down, rubbing his chin in deep thought, then said, "I know of this group, the Tercer Ojo. It means 'third eye.' They work for all the major cartels. They are a sort of intelligence group. Their main objective is to find out if anyone is double-crossing the cartels, or to infiltrate different organisations, sometimes using blackmail or threats to gain advantage. They get information and sort out problems, but I have also heard they are experts on cultural manuscripts and are classed as academic protectors of the cartels."

He went on. "It all makes sense now! That is why Ben was being so suspicious about where he found the parchment and who his sponsors were. But you're right, his life is in danger. These guys are a mean bunch and will surely kill him, as they probably would have done had he found what they are looking for, for fear he would talk: But, they will not kill him if they think he is lying about not finding it, and that he has stashed it somewhere. They will try to get him to tell them where it is. We have to try and find him."

He then told Blanca to go home, get her things, and go stay with family away from Pisté, as they may come looking for her, to use her to get Ben to talk. He gave her a couple of thousand dollars from Ben's bag of money, and then took her phone number so he could contact her to get an update on the situation. Before she left he asked her if Ben had told his "dodgy sponsors" that we had joined him on the dig.

Through Crystal Clear *Waters*

She answered, "No, Mr Dusty, he was supposed to do it alone. But if they ask any of the men that helped Ben on the dig, they are bound to tell them. Be careful, Mr Dusty."

Dusty told Blanca not to worry and to be assured we would endeavour to find Ben. Blanca thanked us and left. We decided to go back to the site one last time in the morning and search deeper into the bush around the ruins, figuring Ben may have gone into hiding.

Daylight broke, and we headed off to the ruins, leaving the car behind in town and walking, as Dusty said it would be safer that way. We went deep into the bush, ringing Ben's cell phone again. This time we could hear it ringing and quickly ran in the direction of the sound. In a clearing, just over a pile of rocks, we could see Ben's backpack and tent roll and scurried to where they were. Ben's phone was lying on the ground, and there were signs of a struggle. We found a small amount of blood on a stone a few feet away from his backpack. We searched around the area, trying to pick up which way his kidnappers had gone. I found a screwed-up piece of paper and called Dusty to take a look. He opened up the paper and read aloud what was written:

Zama – City of Dawn - 20° 12'53 North - 87° 44' West

I asked him what it meant, and he told me it was a location in Quintana Roo called Tulum. "Come on, Chi, let's get back, pick up the car, and go to Tulum." Dusty hid our passports, papers, and the bag containing the money under the floorboards, saying we should leave our clothes and bags here, to make anyone that came looking for us think we were still here. And off we went, leaving Pisté, travelling to Valladolid and on to Chemax, finally arriving in Tulum.

It was a beautiful town, facing east towards the Caribbean Sea. Now a tourist attraction, it used to be an important obsidian trade hub, with routes to both land and sea. Today, tourists came to see the ruins of the temple, which was once the site for the worship of the Descending, or Divine God.

"Let's find a room to stay in, and then we can take a look around," said Dusty. There were plenty of "room to let" signs in the windows of the side streets, so it didn't take long to get somewhere to stay. On going into the room we just flopped back on the beds, exhausted from the events of the last few days.

I asked Dusty if he had a plan. He replied, "Not exactly. We are just gonna have to play it by ear. But right now, we are out of cigarettes, so you stay here and I'll go get some. Back in a tick."

Through Crystal Clear *Waters*

Dusty left, and I just lay back on the bed. I had no idea how we were going to handle this. I had been in some scrapes in the past, but this was like something out of a movie.

I got off the bed and boiled the kettle to make a coffee. Hearing the door open, I called out, "That didn't take long."

Suddenly, I was grabbed from behind by a Mexican man who put his hand over my mouth. I struggled, trying to fight him off, but when he swung me round, I could see a second man, pointing a gun at me. I stopped struggling. They took me down the back stairs, bundling me into the back of a black van, slamming the doors shut, and driving off. I sat up and saw Dusty lying on the van floor, with blood coming out of a wound on his forehead. I tore a bit of my shirt off and tried to clean the wound whilst trying to wake Dusty. After a few moments, he said, "Ouch! That hurts, what happened, Chi?" I told him what had just occurred. Dusty held his head and told me; "I had just got the cigs and was on my way back when, *wham*. Didn't remember a thing till you woke me up. They must have watched Ben's car and followed us here."

"Where do you think they are taking us?" I asked.

"How the hell should I know, Chi?" he snapped. As soon as the words left his mouth, he apologised, telling me he felt bad for having got me involved. I told him not to worry about that and to just concentrate on finding a way out of this shit. He advised me, when they started asking questions, to just plead ignorant, telling them I knew nothing and had only been helping out on a Mayan dig. If they asked my name, I was to make one up. I must not give my real one—that was why he had hidden our passports.

Dusty then reverted back to his usual composure, laughed, and said, "Well, at least I got the cigs before they wacked me. Want a fag, Chi?" I took a cigarette, giving him a look I would give one of my children when they had done something stupid. But the joviality of the moment did not erase the fact that we were in deep trouble. We needed to get away from these people. We spent the rest of the time in the van trying to come up with solutions. However, we wouldn't know the extent of what we were involved in until we reached our destination. What we did know was that they had guns.

It seemed to take an eternity before the van stopped. They opened the doors, shouting, "Out, out!" Four men, each waving guns at us, ushered us through a door to which seemed like a large metal warehouse in the middle of nowhere. They took us to the back, pushing us into a small room, bolting the door as they left. Looking around the room, there was a table with three chairs on one side of the room and some small barred windows, high up towards the ceiling. Dusty pulled the table under one of the windows and climbed up to look. He said he could see one of the men talking on a cell phone. The other three were laughing and joking, passing round a bottle they were taking in turns drinking from. We checked out the room, which didn't present any way of escaping, so we just sat smoking a cigarette. We knew the only way we would be able to make a move was if someone came in and we jumped them, or they moved us from here.

About an hour or so later we heard a vehicle approach. Dusty jumped up on the table again to see what was happening, but he couldn't see anything. We could hear voices, but couldn't make out what they were talking about. Ten minutes later, the door opened. Our hearts were pounding as we heard the sound of the large bolts slamming open. Two men entered. We could see guns stuffed into their trouser belts, so thought it unwise to try anything.

One of the men stood by the door. The other one, who was tall, quite fat, and obviously in charge, pulled up a chair to the centre of the room and sat down. As we stood there, watching the seated man, he growled, "What do you know of the crystal, gringos?"

Kidnapped

"What crystal?" Dusty answered. "I don't know what you're on about."

The man got up, walked across to Dusty, slapping him across the face, saying, "You came to help your friend find the crystal. Where is it?" Dusty looked back at the man, telling him he had only joined his friend on an archaeological dig to find Mayan artefacts, which didn't include any crystals. The man told Dusty he was lying and shouted to the other man to go get him.

A few minutes later, two guys came in, dragging a very bruised and battered Ben. I was scared and shocked to see the state he was in. They threw him onto the ground at our feet, telling him to talk. Ben looked up at Dusty, pleading with him to tell them anything he knew. Dusty thought quickly and then said, "I don't know what their bloody on about, matey. We never found any crystal at the dig. What's going on Ben?"

Ben looked at me, saying, "I'm begging you. Remember the parchment I found?" I looked across at Dusty, remembering what he had told me in the van about pleading ignorant. I replied, "I never saw you find any parchment. We just found pottery and obsidian. You were busy reading hieroglyphs. There was no sign of any parchment, let alone crystals."

The two men picked Ben up, dragging him towards the door. All the while he was screaming at us to tell them, stating they would kill him if we didn't cooperate.

The man who had asked us questions told us we would remain here until we told them what we knew, and with that they all left, locking the door behind them. Dusty put his finger to his lips, indicating that I keep quiet. He went over and put his ear to the door. They were speaking Spanish, but Dusty could manage to make out a few words before they left the warehouse, and we heard the vehicle take off.

Dusty said they had been talking about whether or not we knew anything and what they should do with us. The guy who had spoken to us had told his men to give us some food, and that he would be back in the morning to have another "chat" with us.

Not long after, the large bolts slammed again and the door opened. While one man pointed a gun at us, another brought a plate with some bread and cold sausage, slinging it on the table along with a couple of cans of Coke. Then they both left.

There was silence; Dusty looked out the window again, reporting he could see two men sitting outside. The van we had been brought in drove off.

I asked Dusty if he thought they would let us go if they believe we didn't know anything. He thought, and after pacing up and down again, told me he didn't trust them and didn't think they would. He said we should be ready to make a move should the opportunity arise and that we should eat the food, as we would need to keep our strength up to get out of there.

We ate the food and then settled down on the floor to wait for the morning. It was cold and scary, but it was no good panicking, so we tried to remain positive. We talked over what they had done to Ben. Dusty said that Ben had got himself involved with these guys and had got paid. He had lied to us, giving us no choice about our part in all this, so we should worry only about ourselves and watch for an opportunity to escape. We thought that if we slept, our minds would be clear in the morning. But try as we may, sleep would not come. The room only had a glimmer of moonlight coming in as darkness fell, and we just sat there smoking nearly all the cigarettes we had. At least we were safe till morning.

Suddenly, we both looked towards the door with our hearts in our mouths. We heard the bolts carefully being released and the door slowly begin to open.

Chapter 18

Dusty's Secret

I could see a familiar face in the glow of the moonlight

"Isaac!" I called out in relief.

He beckoned me and Dusty to follow him, saying, "Shush! Come now."

We followed him out the room, through the warehouse, to the outside. The two men guarding us, were fast asleep on the ground outside the door of the warehouse. Isaac smiled, telling us, "I drugged their bottles." We went with him into the bush, to a clearing where he had an old truck waiting. Clambering into the front, Isaac drove off, not putting the lights on until we reached the main road. He must have driven out of the bush by instinct, as all I could see were flickering shadows as the moonlight danced between the tall trees.

I was happy and relieved that we had escaped a near-impossible situation and thanked Isaac profoundly.

I introduced him to Dusty who said, "Yeah, thanks, matey. I don't know how you did it, or how you knew, but you saved our lives, my friend."

Isaac just nodded and smiled, his eyes fixed firmly on the road ahead. I told Isaac, "I dread to think what would have happened tomorrow when they came back. You should have seen what they did to the other guy we were with. I was really frightened."

Isaac answered, "Me know, but you did well, my child." I smiled to myself, partly because he seemed to be proud of me, but also because he had called me his child. He was more than thirty years younger than me, but I presumed it must be due to his priestly ancestry.

I asked him, "How on Earth did you know where we were?" He said that Izacal had told him three nights ago and that he had come as fast as he could. I wondered how Izacal had known back then, as we were not even in this trouble three days ago. But that didn't matter. All that mattered was we were safe.

I glanced across at Dusty, who was looking puzzled. He knew of Izacal being in my dreams and that he was my spirit guide, but here was Isaac, talking as though he were a real person. Dusty looked me straight in the eyes; his expression was asking "What's this all about?" I just patted his knee, smiling to let him know he shouldn't try to work it out. He shrugged and carried on looking out the window. Dusty often referred to me as his "crazy friend," telling me on many occasions I was weird, but I knew he liked that about me and thought it an endearing part of my character.

As we drove, I could see a road sign that told me we were in a small town called X-Hazil Sur, which was just outside Carrillo Puerto. We headed towards Tixacal and on to Valladolid. From there, the next stop was Pisté.

I was a bit confused when Isaac asked me if I knew what I should do with the crystal. Turning to him, I said, "We didn't find the crystal."

Isaac looked at me, then at Dusty. "Oh, I see. But when you do have the crystal, you will know what to do with it. Izacal will instruct you." I looked across to see Dusty's reaction to what Isaac had said, but he just kept looking out the window. I assumed he had not heard. I was going to ask Isaac what he meant when he cut in. "You need to get all the things you left behind in Pisté and go straight back to the States. You can take this truck to the airport, and I will meet up with you later." I knew when Isaac cut in to any of my questions; it meant "don't ask." So I just told him okay, glancing at Dusty, who now had his eyes shut and I presumed him to be asleep.

We drove the rest of the way to Pisté in silence. Isaac parked the truck a few yards from the room where our possessions were. We got out and he handed Dusty the keys, saying, "Take care." I turned round to thank Isaac, but he had disappeared.

"Where did he go?" asked Dusty, looking all around.

"Don't worry," I told him "He does that all the time. One minute he's there, the next he's gone."

"Well I'm sure glad he turned up when he did," Dusty mused. "He's a strange sort of chap, but he totally saved our bacon."

I just grabbed him by his arm, saying, "Come on, let's go get our bags and passports and get out of here."

We retrieved our stuff from the room, with Dusty stashing Ben's large bundle of dollars in every pocket and crevice he could hide it in, then got into the truck, and set off. I was just thanking God we were finally leaving, when I realised Dusty was driving to Chichen Itza. "What are you doing?" I asked him. "We need to go to Cancun."

He said he needed to check something out at the site.

"Are you mad?" I retorted. "What if they are watching the place?"

Dusty's Secret

Dusty turned to me and smiled. "Gotta be done, Chi. Trust me."

I knew it would do no good to argue, but I couldn't help but think that trusting him was what got me into all this drama.

When we got to the site, Dusty went into the bush, sticking his hand into the hollow of a tree. He retrieved something wrapped up in an old piece of hessian sacking.

"What the heck have you got there?" I enquired.

"Later, Chi. Let's get going. I will tell you on the way." He hurried me to the truck to head off for Cancun. Dusty drove like a herd of bulls were chasing him. I tried to get out of him what he had in the sackcloth, but he just kept saying, "wait." Curiosity was killing me.

We didn't stop till we reached a coffeehouse just outside Cancun. Dusty went in and brought two coffees out for us to drink in the truck. He took the bundle out of his inside pocket, and I eagerly watched as he started to unwrap it.

I couldn't believe my eyes when he placed in my hands a beautiful piece of quartz crystal, exquisitely shaped into a pyramid. Each side measured approximately four inches, with a weight of about four pounds.

Through Crystal Clear *Waters*

I held this spectacular object in my hand, hardly believing we were in possession of something of this magnitude. My heart was pounding. I had never felt anything like it, other than when my grandson was born and placed into my hands. "Dusty," I gasped. "Explain."

He told me he had found it on his first swim underwater to the cave. The crystal had given off rays of rainbow light in the dimly lit cavern, leading him to find the skeleton in the rocklike cradle formation. It was as if the priest had died holding the crystal. He decided to keep it quiet. His time spent alone with Ben, before we had broke through to the cache, hadn't given him any confidence in him. His reluctance to divulge who his sponsors were, along with his convenient memory lapse on where he had found the parchment, had convinced Dusty that if Ben was keeping his cards close to his chest, so would he. Dusty felt Ben had only been using him for his knowledge of cultures, and given what had happened since, he now believed Ben had no conscience about our safety. He also felt that, had it been Ben who had found the crystal, all our lives would be probably in considerably more danger. Having the knowledge that the crystal even existed might mean a death sentence.

I asked Dusty if he thought the Tercer Ojo knew who we were.

"I really don't think so, Chi. Ben has only ever known me by my nickname, even when we were in the mob together, and he doesn't know you at all, only that I call you Chi. So I think we're safe there. The helpers on the dig only speak Spanish, so all they would know would be that a couple of gringos were with Ben on the dig."

"Thank God for that," I said.

As I sat there holding the crystal, I could feel a warmth creep over my whole body as the crystal started to glow. Dusty looked shocked, saying "whats happening Chi? You have a golden light all around you." I told him I realy didn't understand it, but I had a feeling of emense power and instructed Dusty to take my hand.

A soon as we touched, he too was surrounded by the light. We sat there for about five minutes holding hands until the glow from the crystal began to fade. "Wow!" said Dusty, "That was unreal, I felt better than I have ever felt in my whole life, and I got this feeling that me and you were as one." He looked at me and concluded, "That was something not from this world".

Following an experience like that, I would have thought we would have both been scared out of our wits, but the exact opposite was the case. I felt both exhilarated and strong, and as we both sat there staring silently at each other, I knew that Dusty felt the same way.

Dusty stressed we needed to leave Mexico as soon as possible. He wrapped the crystal pyramid in the cloth, putting it back in his pocket, and we continued into Cancun.

When we got to the airport, Dusty gave me the crystal and told me he would go to check in first, to make sure no one was looking for us. I should wait until I saw him walk away with his boarding pass in his hand. Then I would know it was safe to continue. He said we would be on separate seats on the plane and should keep a safe distance from each other until we reached the States.

I watched as Dusty got his boarding pass, placed the crystal in my luggage and after a few minutes went to check in myself. But it wasn't until the plane thundered down the runway at Houston that I felt the pressure was off. As I descended down the steps to terra firma, I gave a huge sigh of relief. We went separately through security, and I caught up with Dusty in the car park. As we got into his Jeep to drive home, we looked at each other and smiled. We could finally relax.

On the way back, we stopped to fill up with gas and get a drink. After I visited the ladies' room and got back in the Jeep, Dusty handed me a newspaper, saying; "Look at this." On the front page of *The Houston Chronicle* was a horrifying picture of a bruised and battered Ben. The headline read, "ANOTHER FOREIGN TOURIST BECOMES VICTIM OF THE TERCER OJO CARTEL IN MEXICO."

I turned to look at Dusty. His steel-blue poker eyes showed no emotion. "I'm sorry," I said. "I know he was your friend." Dusty just looked me straight in the eyes and said, "Hey, you live a lie, you die a liar. Ultimately, Ben turned out to be a friend only to himself."

I never had liked Ben very much and had been angered by all the trouble he had put us through. But now, a big lump came in my throat, and tears filled my eyes. It deeply saddened me to see the horrible way he had met his death. No one deserved to be treated that way. A feeling of guilt filled my heart when I remembered the look in his eyes in that room in the warehouse, as he pleaded with us to save his life. I wondered if there was anything more we could have done, or if we should have told Isaac to rescue Ben, too. Deep down, I knew that had not been an option. But the image of his pleading eyes would haunt me all my life.

Chapter 19

Izacal Returns

We were both shattered by the time we reached Dusty's house. I was looking forward to a decent night's sleep, something I had not done in almost a week.

After sitting down with a beer, I unwrapped the crystal pyramid, placing it on the coffee table in front of us. We both just sat staring at this magnificent object for quite a while.

"What the hell do we do now?" Dusty asked.

I knew we had to get it to the right person, but at that moment no solution presented itself. "To be quite honest, I haven't got a clue," I told him.

We chatted for a while about the events that had taken place in the last week. While talking about Ben, I noticed Dusty seemed very uneasy. He told me he didn't really want to think about what had happened to him. He stressed that although he felt sorry for the man, he believed he had made the right decision, since his friendship with Ben had proved false in the end. He knew that if he had let him know about the crystal, the three of us would be dead right now. I asked Dusty if he thought those Tercer Ojo people had given up on finding us, and if Ben's death had put a close to the matter. He thought it probably had, but to be on the safe side, we should remain cautious until we had got rid of the crystal.

I was shocked by this comment. "What do you mean, get rid of? We have to get it to its rightful keeper!"

Dusty huffed, replying, "I'm not being rude, Chi, but neither of us knows where to begin. I can't see we have a hope in hell of finding this so-called keeper. That is, if he even exists."

"I know, I know! But we can't give up now; especially after all we have gone through. Look, we are both tired. Maybe we will think clearer in the morning. Don't give up on me now, Dusty." I could see his point, but something told me we would find a way. Dusty was the risk-taking, adventurous one, and I was sure he would take on the task.

"Have I ever given up on you before, Chi?" he asked. "You're right. Let's get some kip and think about what to do after that."

Izacal Returns

We said good-night. I took the crystal pyramid up to my room, placing it on the dresser, then put on my PJs and lay down in my comfortable bed. The moonlight coming through the window seemed to home in on the crystal, sending rainbow waves of light that danced on the ceiling. I snuggled down and lay there watching the spectacular display, until my eyes closed and I drifted off into a well-earned sleep.

But I soon began to dream. I was sitting on a rock high on a hilltop, overlooking a large canyon, watching an eagle circling round in front of me. I turned my head when I heard footsteps approaching and saw Izacal walking towards me, saying. "Greetings, my daughter."

As he sat down beside me, I noticed he looked much younger than the last time I had seen him in dreamtime. "You are aging well, Izacal," I remarked.

He just smiled and said; "Age is like time, it's irrelevant." I joked with him that he could have let me have at least one night's sleep before dreaming me, but this made him angry. "Don't be flippant, child! This is no joke. Do you not yet see what is happening?"

"Of course I do!" I replied. "I have been through hell and back because of this crystal, but what am I supposed to do with it now?"

Through Crystal Clear Waters

Izacal smiled, patting my hand. "That's why I am here now. You must do what you told your friend—get it to its rightful keeper."

I looked him square in the eyes and said, "Can't I just give it to Isaac? He will know what to do."

He gave me a sympathetic look. "My dear child, the crystal is your responsibility. It has always been your destiny to deliver the crystal. Don't worry your head. I will tell you what you need to do. Isaac will soon help you, near to the time you reach the elders that are waiting for your arrival."

I asked Izacal if he could tell me what information the crystal pyramid held. He told me only the Keeper could do that and that I would find out about the information later, when my journey was complete.

But he could tell me what the purpose of it was. He spoke of what the parchment had told and why it was necessary to charge the crystal with the energy of the words of the ancients. He said it was foretold that all the native peoples of the world, would be, over time, stripped of their heritage, beliefs, customs, and even their languages. This would happen not just in South America, but in every corner of the Earth. If they had not protected their teachings and prophesies, they would be lost forever, and so too would be the future and well-being of humanity. He reminded me of what Isaac had taught me of Atlantis and that the same thing was happening again. The unbalance of good and evil was threatening the whole of mankind. Now was the time of awakening. This crystal, along with many others around the world, was part of this transition.

I asked Izacal, how they were able to forsee so far into the future.

He spoke of how the high priests and elders received their knowledge. They would cultivate and harvest coca leaves, dry them out in the sun, and grind them. They mixed the ground leaves with the ashes of limestone and the quinoa plant, to enhance a feeling of euphoria, enabling them to go into a trance-like state. The priests also made a tea with the leaves and would read leaves left in the drinking vessel, in a form of divination. Besides the religious ceremonies, the leaves were used in traditional medicine and were known to treat a number of illnesses, from nosebleeds and ulcers to rheumatism, asthma, and digestive problems. They were also used as an anaesthetic and an aphrodisiac. The leaders gave a lesser strength of coca to the people to chew, as it helped overcome tiredness, hunger, and thirst, enabling both workers and warriors to endure longer periods at their tasks.

Through Crystal Clear Waters

The seeds of the coca plant, along with cocoa and tobacco, had been brought to Earth by Izacal's ancestors from another of the thirteen planets and planted on Turtle Island. These plants were widely used in Atlantis, so when the twelve Planet Trackers and Star Keepers left Atlantis along with their crystals, they took leaves and seeds of the plants with them to help them on their journey and planted them at their new locations all over the world.

When the Spanish invaded the native peoples of South America, they recognised the value of the coca leaves and took them back to their leaders. The leaves were often exchanged as gifts amongst world leaders, nobility, and religious figures, and used by powerful people to this very day. Governments, scientists, and inventors have all used the power of the coca leaf, which led to great leaps in the West—from the Industrial Revolution, to advances in medicine and weapon design, to human space travel. Many great men in human history used coca—Einstein, Leonardo da Vinci, and Nostradamus, to name but a few. They used it to open their minds to awareness of what could be. But some used it for power and profit and made the growing of the plant illegal, for fear the people would realise all the lies their leaders had been telling them for years. Over time coca was corrupted by experimenting with different alkali mixes and processed into a destructive drug called cocaine. Leaders would use cocaine to prime their armies for war, because this new form, as well as preventing tiredness and hunger, also desensitised the soldiers, so that they had no conscience about killing innocent people. A group of soldiers, after leaving the military in the early 1900s, took this formula and started processing it in Colombia. They would make money by selling it to everyday people. Since the new form caused addiction, they made a lot of money as demand for the drug grew. This was the start of the drug cartels. They became powerful and started corrupting the drug even more, cutting the drug with all sorts of substances to make it go further. They processed it so it could be snorted as a white powder up the nose, mixed with water to be injected into the blood, or placed in a tablet-like form called "crack" that could be broken down and smoked. These processes made billions of dollars for the cartels. The learned ones of the cartels had the parchment that told about the crystal and the information it held about the intended purpose of coca and are fearful that if the true form was to become available, it would put an end to their profitable empire.

"That's why they kidnapped you," finished Izacal. "They needed to know if the crystal had been found, and they would do anything to stop the information getting out."

Had we declared finding the crystal, he added, that would have caused trouble too, since the governments were also fearful of the truth. If people had access to the true form, they would become aware, and civil war would break out all over the world. No more would people listen to their religious leaders. They would go back to ancient beliefs. The fact is, he said, that today just 1 per cent of the population owned more than 40 per cent of global assets. If people found out the truth, no government, bankers, large company directors or anyone in power, including the cartels, would be safe from civil unrest. This was happening already in the Middle East, with people standing up to dictatorships. A few forms of these awakening drugs were available, like Coca-Cola and Red Bull, but the quantities in those refined products, only enhanced the "feel-good factor," just like chocolate, and posed no threat at all.

In the early '60s, Izacal continued, governments became worried about the hippie movement, New Agers, and student protests at the dawning of the Age of Aquarius. Leaders made the taking of drugs illegal, for fear of awareness. But the drug industry just went underground, and the drugs bought on the streets today were corrupted and addictive. The powers that be let the people have chocolate and tobacco, just to keep the equilibrium. But with more people "waking up," they were now trying to restrict tobacco in an attempt to control the masses.

Next, Izacal said, I was to learn of the 2012 fear we were all being fed. He told me he was both amused and saddened by all the hype about prophesies of 2012, which were being perpetuated through the media. He believed this was purposely done as a way to control the people, by striking fear about what may happen. The doomsday predictions were backed by statements from scientists, so the people would believe all the rubbish. It has had a dramatic effect, he said, with some people wishing to commit suicide or kill their entire families to protect their children from suffering. We were told this all comes from the fourth cycle of the Mayan calendar, which supposedly states the end of the Earth will take place on December 12, 2012. This was *not* what the Mayans predicted, he said. They did talk about great devastations which would inevitably take place, like earthquakes, volcanic eruptions and tsunamis, but did not give a date for the end of the world.

The media told us a comet may strike the Earth, solar flares would wipe us out, or that the Earth would tilt off its axis. They referred to the galactic alignment at the time of the winter solstice, when the Earth, the sun, and the Milky Way would be in perfect alignment, and that this would end in disaster.

But the truth was, it signified the ending of the astrological Age of Pisces, announcing the beginning of the Age of Aquarius—the age of humanity. So therefore, when a new fifth cycle began, it would be the time of awakening.

Chapter 20

Izacal's Instructions

Izacal told me what I should do for the next step of my journey, to get the crystal to its rightful keeper. He said, "You will meet with Chief Soaring Eagle of the Tsalagi tribe, here in Texas. They know you have the crystal, but they will probably test you before they let you into their confidence. The name Tsalagi is the original common tribal name for those you now know as the Cherokee."

I was very excited at the prospect of meeting with the tribe and actual chief of the Cherokee. "Cool that sounds great! I didn't even know there were any Cherokee Indians around here."

"They are very wary of outsiders," Izacal replied. "They are a matriarchal society, so it will probably be better if you go alone to this first meeting. And as I said before, you will be tested."

"What sort of test?" I asked him.

Through Crystal Clear Waters

He told me they would want to know my character and what I knew of their ancient beliefs, as well as my reaction to certain things they would tell me. This would help them decide if I was of the right spiritual nature to be tested. He said, "If they test you, it will be to prove your courage and purity of heart. Pass the test, then you and Dusty will be accepted and be invited by the chief to attend a powwow and to make plans for your journey." As to what the actual test would be, he couldn't tell me, as that would depend on what the elders of the tribe said after my interview.

It all sounded very intriguing, but I said to Izacal, "I know very little about the history of the Cherokee, so will I fail the test? And what happens if I fail?"

Izacal smiled and said, "No, my child, you will not fail. This is your destiny and I have complete faith in you. I will teach you what you need to know for your initial meeting, and I am sure they will fill you in with the rest of their beliefs after the test."

So I waited patiently for him to tell me the story of the Cherokee, a tribe from the Iroquoian family, who used to live in the mountain region of South Alleghenies, part of the Appalachian Mountain range. The name Cherokee was an English adaption of their name and the one they presently went by. The Portuguese called them "Chalaque" and the

Izacal's Instructions

French used the name "Chiriquí." The name Tsalagi probably came from the Choctaw, from "Chilwk-ki" meaning "cave people." The Cherokee originally called themselves "'Ani'-Yŭn'-wiyd," meaning "real people." Their northern family, the Iroquois, called them "Oyata'ge'ronon," which means "inhabitants of the cave country."

There were once fourteen clans, but today there were just seven, which were as follows:

1. Ani'-wa' a — Wolf
2. Ani'Tsi'skwa — Bird
3. Ani'-Kawĭ — Deer
4. Ani'-Sah'a'ni — Blue
5. Ani'-wi'di — Red Paint
6. Ani'-Ga'tagewi — Wild Potato
7. Ani'-Igilohi — Long Hair

The number seven was a very important number to the Cherokee, said Izacal, representing the utmost of sacredness and purity. The seven clans were mentioned in their ritual prayers, having a connection with the seven "mother towns" of the clans. The Owl and the Cougar attained this level of sacredness in their ancient beliefs and were honoured because they were the only two species to remain awake through the seven days and nights of creation. Another special number was four, representing not only the four cardinal directions, but also the elemental forces of earth, wind, fire, and water. The tribe also honoured certain trees, including cedar, pine, spruce, laurel, and holly. These trees did not shed their leaves and were therefore considered to be important in the story of creation.

Izacal went on to tell me that I must never touch any of the Cherokee's sacred objects which, after ceremonial use, were wrapped in either deerskin or white cloth and stored in a box. The sacred circle was also something to be respected, and I must never enter it unless invited to do so. In their ceremonies, the tribe constructed a "council house", by using branches and binding them together, blessing it by lighting a fire. The Stomp Dance was usually performed by the tribal women, where they dance around the council house in an anticlockwise sacred circle. The women's drum, he said, must also never be touched unless by invitation. No decisions were made without first consulting the women elders. The medicine man was still revered. They believed good is rewarded and evil is punished, and they were cautious of people using "evil medicine" against them. This could be people wishing them harm or failure, so they were therefore very suspicious of outsiders coming to their ceremonies.

He then gave me a contact number for Chief Soaring Eagle, telling me to give her a call in the morning and that she was expecting me.

"A woman?" I asked Izacal. I had expected that the chief would be a man.

He replied, "Yes, child. Remember I told you they were a matriarchal society. Women deal with women and men deal with men. Although at your first meeting you will be met and invited in by the chief, who is a woman, there will also be a couple of male elders there, too."

I asked Izacal if I should take the crystal to this meeting. He told me they would not want to see it yet, so I should not take it. But before I left the tribe, I should ask the chief for something to wrap and carry it in, and that once I had wrapped the crystal, it should not be taken out until our final destination was reached and I had delivered it into the hands of the Keeper. Then all would be revealed. Izacal said, "Sleep now child." And he was gone.

I woke up straight after the dream and wanted to wake Dusty up to tell him what I had learnt, but I thought better of it after glancing at the clock. It was 3:30 a.m., so I scribbled the telephone number down on a scrap of paper before lying back down to try to get back to sleep. I lay awake for a time, so excited to get to meet the Cherokee, and wondered where we would have to travel to find the Keeper. But in the end, tiredness took over and I drifted off.

Chapter 21

The Test

Awaking at five in the morning, I could not contain my excitement about what Izacal had told me. Jumping out of bed, grabbing the piece of paper with the telephone number on it, I rushed across the landing, knocking on Dusty's bedroom door. He didn't answer, but I could hear him snoring, so I opened the door, went over, and shook him, telling him to wake up.

"Chi, what's wrong?" Dusty mumbled. I told him nothing was wrong. I just wanted to tell him I know what we must do next with the crystal. "Oh good," he said and rolled over in an attempt to go back to sleep.

I shook him again, saying; "Get up, Dusty! Izacal told me what we do next!"

He begrudgingly sat up, moaning, "Can't it wait? I suppose it's no good arguing with you when you're in this mood. Make me a coffee and I'll be downstairs in a minute."

"Okay," I replied and made us coffee.

Dusty came downstairs and sat on the armchair, saying, "This had better be good, to get me out of bed at this unearthly hour!"

I gave him his drink and began to tell him about my dream and what Izacal had told me about meeting a Cherokee chief. I handed him the piece of paper with the telephone number on it, waiting for his response.

He looked at the number, then at me, and said, "You know if it was anyone else but you that expected me to act on a dream, I would tell them to get lost. But we will give this number a ring and see what happens. But Chi, you can't ring this early. Wait a couple of hours at least."

I thought for a moment, realising he was right. I answered, "Sure, I was just excited. Are you not just a little bit excited, Dusty?"

He started laughing, lit up a cigarette, and said, "Probably will be when I've drank my coffee. You are crazy, Chi! But that's what I like about you."

I went to get the crystal pyramid so we could have one last look at it before having to wrap it for its journey. We both admired its beauty and craftsmanship. Dusty got out his magnifying glass and said he could not define any visible signs of any tools used to shape its form. He asked me if we would find out what information the crystal held, once we had handed it to its keeper. I told him Izacal had given me the impression that we would, because he had said "everything would be revealed." We mused over what the revelations would be about the fifth calendar, and what the information might tell us about drugs.

When I told him that Izacal had told me the Cherokee knew I was coming and that it was my destiny, Dusty again began laughing uncontrollably. After he composed himself, he said; "It's a privilege to be in your presence, Lady Chi. Are you sure you want an old sea dog like me to accompany you on your destiny?"

I folded my arms indignantly. "Shut up, Dusty. I am only telling you what Izacal told me, so stop making fun of me. Don't forget it was you who rang me up in the early hours to come with you in the first place."

Still laughing, he apologised for upsetting me. "You got to admit, Chi, it *is* funny, and a bit farfetched. But don't worry; I am with you all the way, no matter what happens next. I am beginning to feel like Indiana Jones."

I took the crystal back up to my room, took a shower, and got dressed. When I came back downstairs, Dusty had cooked a full English breakfast. He told me it was a peace offering and besides, we needed to keep our strength up for our journey. We tucked into bacon, sausage, egg, mushrooms, and beans, with several slices of fried bread and a glass of fresh orange juice. It was a feast after last week's events not allowing any time for a proper meal, and it helped pass the time before ringing the chief.

After eating, we sat down, ready to ring the number. Dusty asked me if I knew what I was going to say to whoever answered the phone. I told him I was just going to play it by ear. I put the phone on loudspeaker and began dialling. I was nervous as I heard it ringing, wondering what this person would say—or what I was going to say that would make any sense, for that matter.

A woman's voice answered. I enquired if she was Chief Soaring Eagle and was so relieved when the reply was "yes." Explaining that I had the crystal and had been given her phone number to arrange a meeting, she replied, "Ah yes, you must be Chiane."

I glanced across at Dusty, who just sat there, mouth open, looking completely astonished. After confirming I was Chiane, she asked if we could get to the far end of the lake by 10:30 a.m. Dusty was nodding his head, so I told her we could. She went on to say that when we pulled off the road we would see a big gate with a red cloth tied to it. On arriving, we should give

The Test

her a call and she would come and unlock the gate and let us in. I told her okay, and she hung up.

I replaced the receiver, and Dusty and I sat staring at each other. He must have been shocked, as this was his first time experiencing the effects of my dreams. A few moments passed before Dusty asked, "Are you ready for this, Chi?"

"Ready or not, I don't really think we have a choice."

Dusty showered and dressed, and then we got into the Jeep, heading for the far side of the lake. We pulled up at the gate with the red cloth and took a look around. Through the trees and bush we could see a wooden building, like a single-story house with a veranda near the edge of the lake. There were several cars parked outside.

"Let's do it," said Dusty, so I rang the chief from my cell phone. She said she would be there in a minute, and sure enough, a car pulled up to the other side of the gate. The chief got out, unlocked, and opened it, gesturing with her hand for us to enter. We drove in, and she locked the gate behind us and told us to follow her down to the building.

In my head, I had expected to see someone in traditional Indian attire, complete with headdress, but the chief just looked like a normal woman. We parked up and got out of the Jeep. She came over to us and smiling, shook our hands, inviting us into the house, offering us food and drink. Not wanting to be impolite, we took a piece of cake and a can of Coke, sitting down with the chief at one of the rows of tables and benches that filled about one-third of the room. The rest of the room was a kitchen area, with sink, stove, and fridge. There was also a large table displaying both hot food and snacks. There were a few other people at another table chatting, they looked up and smiled at us when we entered.

I introduced myself and Dusty to the chief. She told us we could call her Dawn, as this was her American name, and said she would need to talk to me with two elders when they arrived. Dusty, though, would have to wait.

We sat making general conversation until two men came into the building. One was in his mid-thirties, wearing a brightly coloured tunic and blue jeans, with his long, fair hair tied back in a plait down his back. The other was an older man, probably in his seventies, in brown trousers, a black-and-white checked shirt and moccasins, dark hair, and many age lines on his face. The chief signalled them to join us and after greetings, I went with the three of them to a table at the far side of the room. I turned round to Dusty. He smiled and put his thumb up to assure me.

The Test

The chief asked me to tell them about myself, which I proceeded to do. They seemed particularly interested in the fact that I had no family background and had always been guided by dreams. They became quite excited when I told them of the dream I had had while in Jamaica—of a gathering of people from around the world, about the twelve Star Keepers and Planet Trackers holding up their crystals on a rock, and the Cherokee chief that had given a speech.

Then they asked how I had found the crystal. I related all the events since landing in Mexico, telling them it was Dusty who had found it, hiding it due to his suspicions about Ben, and then giving it to me. I also told them of the horrible death of Ben.

They chatted amongst themselves for a few minutes and then asked me what I knew about the Cherokee Nation. I relayed to them bits and pieces of what Izacal had taught me, and they seemed quite impressed with my knowledge.

The chief then told me about the Trail of Tears. This was the story of how the whites discovered gold in Northern Georgia and, becoming possessed with gold fever, they turned on the Cherokee. The government told the tribes they had to leave their land, farms, and homes. She told of how President Andrew Jackson had defied the US Supreme Court, who had made a ruling in favour of those who stood by the Cherokee, defending them by speaking out against displacement and affirming the Cherokee's sovereignty. The US government justified Jackson's orders using the Treaty of New Echota in 1835. The Cherokee, by signing the treaty, would give up their land and homes in exchange for new land in the Indian Territory, given a promise of money, livestock, and provisions. This caused a split between those who signed the treaty and those who opposed it, leading to fighting and many deaths. It gave the government a justifiable reason to forcibly remove almost all of the seventeen thousand Cherokee from their homelands. During this removal, an estimated four thousand lost their lives, either through hunger and disease or by being killed. This became known as the Trail of Tears.

After I had listened to all they had to tell me of their history, beliefs, and myths, they told me to sit with Dusty while they discussed my test. Dusty and I went outside to have a cigarette and waited. We discussed that every culture had a similar story of oppression, and wondered if it would be possible to change the way humans treated each other. One thing we did know, was that we were both a part of something that we were destined to see through to the end.

After about twenty minutes, they came back, beckoning us both to follow them. We went to a clearing

The Test

about fifty yards from the building, where I saw twelve large ceramic pots. Parchment had been tied onto the tops so I could not see what was inside them. In front of each of the pots, which were set out in a circle, rather like a clock face, were cards, with the numbers one to twelve.

Dusty sat down on the ground with the two male elders, while the chief led me into the centre of the circle of pots. She told me this was a test of "strength of courage and purity of heart," and that in one of the pots was an eagle feather. In all the others were fire ants. She instructed me to make a choice as to which one contained the feather, put my hand through the parchment into the pot, take out the feather, and present it to her. She told me to take my time and went and sat down with the others.

I stood there looking at the circle of pots. The elders were all watching me intently. Dusty had a concerned look on his face, and I must admit I was extremely nervous. What would happen if I failed this test? Would they not help get the crystal to the Keeper? I put these thoughts out of my head and concentrated on my task. I remembered Izacal had told me the number seven was their most sacred number, so surely they would have put the feather in that pot. If I was wrong, I would be badly bitten by the ants, so I had to get it right. I went over to the seventh pot and was just about to push my hand into it, but then something inside me said "no." I took a step back.

I thought about what Izacal had said about the Stomp Dance, that the women moved in a circle in an anticlockwise direction, one only practiced by the Cherokee. If I viewed the pots from that perspective, the number seven would be in the fifth position. I began to shake. I had to make a choice, so stepping to the number five pot; I took a deep breath, plunging my hand through the parchment.

Eureka! I had got it right. It was such a relief I pulled out the eagle feather and handed it to the chief. Dusty clapped his hands and the two elders got up and started dancing and chanting. The chief thanked me and said we must make plans. I did as Izacal told me, asking her for something in which to wrap and carry the crystal. She went off, returning with a piece of white cloth and a deerskin pouch. She told me I must wrap the crystal in the cloth and place it in the pouch, and there it should remain until I handed it to the Keeper. She asked me who had touched the crystal. I told her only Dusty and I. The chief then instructed me I must cleanse the crystal by burying it in the earth for seven days before I wrap it. At the end of the seven days we would make the journey to the Keeper.

The Test

I asked where we would be travelling to and was told a place called Asheville, Tennessee, in the southeastern United States. We would take the trade path across the Appalachian Mountains, so we should wear appropriate clothing and footwear for the journey. The younger of the two elders was also to make this trip along with the chief. His name was Daniel, or to use his tribal name, Chief Wandering Bear. Daniel was a warrior chief, and it would be he that picked us up for the journey. Chief Soaring Eagle told us again that it would be a lot easier if we called her by her known name of Dawn, rather than keep calling her chief. She was happy to have Dusty accompany us on the journey, as she had seen he had given me much support and had shown great wisdom in the decision he had made about concealing the crystal. We all sat on the veranda smoking cigarettes, drinking coffee, and chatting.

With all plans laid, it was now time to say our goodbyes. We got in the Jeep and followed Dawn back up to the gate to let us out. Before opening the gate, she came to the Jeep window and gave us both small medicine pouches to wear round our necks at all times to protect us from evil. She also gave me a gift, wrapped in red cloth and tied with a ribbon. I thanked her and she went to unlock the gate. As we drove out, she waved and said, "See you in seven days." Then she locked the gate and drove back to the building. We got back on the road and drove home.

"Well, that was something else!" said Dusty. "How did you know which pot to pick?"

"It was just a hunch, but I was scared I might get the ants."

Dusty said he was glad I chose the right pot and told me to open the gift and see what was inside. I undid the ribbon, opening the cloth to find a beautiful handmade dreamcatcher.

"Oh no," said Dusty. "I hope that doesn't mean you're going to have even more dreams. I had better get ready for more adventures." We both laughed all the way home.

Chapter 22

Journey with the Cherokee

As soon as we reached home, I buried the crystal as instructed. Then going to my room, I hung the dreamcatcher on the headboard and placed the cloth and pouch on the dresser, ready to wrap the crystal once it had been cleansed. When I came downstairs, Dusty had poured me a beer and was sitting with his feet up, drinking rum and counting the huge amount of money he had brought back from Ben's payment.

"Well, Chi," he said, "I never thought I would say this, but you have convinced me with all this dream stuff. I ain't converted to your way of mystical thinking, but I will never doubt you again."

I smiled. "Thank you, kind sir. I have lived with this all my life, and it isn't always easy, you know." My dreams were not something to discuss with just anyone, for fear they would think me crazy or was just making it up. But I had always appreciated his acceptance of my unconventional ways. I told him we mad a good team. After all, he was not your average sort of guy and got himself into all sorts of scrapes. Dusty laughed, telling me he was certainly going to take me along on all of his adventures from now on.

We chatted into the night while watching a documentary on television about the Mayan calendar prophesies. At least we had a whole week to chill out before our next trip. We decided we should take a few days down in San Antonio, with a bit of sightseeing, so Dusty booked a hotel. We planned to leave the day after tomorrow. I thought I had better ring my daughters the next day, to tell them I was okay. I knew I would be in for a telling-off for not ringing them sooner, as it had been over two weeks. With all plans made, we retired for the night. I was hoping I would have a dream-free night and get a sound sleep.

The morning came and I felt quite refreshed, with no dreams. I had slept through till 9:45, so had a good lay in bed. A scrumptious smell of bacon came drifting up the stairs. I got up and went down to find Dusty busy at the stove. After eating, I rang my daughters. Of course, I could not tell them about all that had happened in the last couple of weeks. Instead, I just said I had lost track of time, sorting through all the beautiful artefacts we had found on the dig. They asked when I was coming home, so I told them we were off to another dig where crystals had been found and that I would be home after that. They seemed to accept this new plan, and I convinced myself I had not told an outright lie. It was as near to the truth as I was prepared to give. After catching up with the news back home, and after they had said hello to 'Uncle Dusty', we said our good-byes. Dusty had been listening in, so after I put the phone down, he said to me, "You got out of that one! You had me believing you." I blushed and he laughed.

The next day we were on the road again, travelling to San Antonio. On arriving, we checked into a lovely hotel called La Quinta, dropped our bags, and went for a wander around, taking in the many bars down the River Walk. Over the next few days we swam in the hotel pool, took in the Alamo, did loads of shopping, and ate some glorious food at the many restaurants along the river. It all passed quickly and we were soon headed back home, my bloodstream flowing with tequila from the large quantity of margaritas I had consumed.

Just one day left, then we would be setting off with the chiefs, Dawn and Daniel, for the Appalachian Mountains. We got our backpacks ready, and that evening I dug up the crystal, rinsed the soil off in the lake, and carefully wrapped it in the white cloth, putting it in the pouch and placing it securely in my backpack.

At 9:30 in the morning, Daniel arrived in his Jeep. We set off, picking Dawn up at her home on the way. While we drove, Dawn told us more stories about the Cherokee. We stopped in Louisiana for something to eat before carrying on through Chattanooga, Alabama, and into Tennessee. By this time we had been travelling many hours and it was getting dark, so we drove another fifty miles to The Sleep Inn in Overhill, Tennessee, staying there till midmorning the next day.

Getting back on track, we went on to Hickory, ending up in Ashville, on the boundaries of the Cherokee Nation, located in the Blue Ridge Mountains. The climate there was officially humid subtropical, but it felt quite cool, possibly due to our altitude. We were to take the tourist Jeep into the Blue Ridge National Park. From there, we would be going on foot on the Appalachian Trail, onwards and upwards into the Great Smoky Mountains. Our prime destination was the Qualla Reservation, which was home to many of the Eastern Band of Cherokee, who had remained in the mountains after the Indian Removal Act. They had hid in the mountains while the rest of the Cherokee were forcibly removed to what is now Oklahoma. Those that stayed in the mountains had been led by a warrior called Tsali, and the chief we were heading to see was a descendant of that great warrior chief.

It was a long hard trek across these mountain ranges, but the views and all the different animals and birds were amazing. There were elk and white-tailed deer, and many sightings of wild boar. We saw a few bobcats along the way, thought to be the only remaining wildcat species left in the area, although there had been sightings of mountain lions reported. Happily, we did not come across any. There were plenty of woodpeckers, wild turkeys, and black-capped chickadees, along with yellow-bellied sapsuckers. When we were high on the mountaintops, we sighted quite a lot of golden and bald eagles. The whole trek was very colourful.

While we were in the Rockies, heading for Qualla, we heard the sound of someone crying coming from the bush. The two chiefs wanted to ignore this and carry on our trek, but Dusty had other ideas. Climbing over a fallen tree and some rocks, pushing our way through the bush, we came to a clearing, where a young Indian girl in her early twenties sat on a rock, crying her eyes out.

Dusty went over to her and asked what was wrong. She kept saying "Father is dying," indicating Dusty to follow her. He put his arm around the girl in an

Through Crystal Clear Waters

attempt to calm her down and managed to get her to explain. She told us her father had been bitten by a snake and was dying. The snake was still in the hut, but she could not get to her father as a black bear was outside, blocking her path. We followed her back to the hut and sure enough, there was the bear, prowling around in front of the doorway. Dusty told the girl to wait, telling me to look after her, and started walking slowly towards the bear. I called after him, frightened that he might get attacked, but he just kept going. The bear saw him and stood up on his hind legs, growling and making waving movements with his paws. I was terrified, but then Dusty pulled a gun out of his inside pocket, firing a shot into the air. I was shocked. I didn't even know he had a gun, let alone had brought one along with him. But it did the trick, with the bear sent running into the woods.

The girl hurried to the hut door, shouting for her father, but Dusty stopped her before she went inside. He told her he would check to see if the snake had gone before she went in. He slowly opened the door while I held the girl back, and we could discern a rattling sound coming from within the hut. Dusty attentively stepped inside and moments later, fired another shot. The rattling sound stopped. We all went inside the hut; the snake was dead on the floor. It was a timber rattlesnake, about twenty inches long, greyish-white in colour with black stripes and a yellowish-brown crossband. The girl rushed over to her father, who lay on some blankets at one side of the room. He was an old man who looked like he was in his seventies and try as she may; the girl could not rouse her father. Dusty checked him out, determining he was dead and had probably died from a heart attack rather than the snakebite. The girl was inconsolable, but Dusty managed to persuade her to come with us to the reservation, where we could get help to fetch her father from the hut. So we covered the old man with a blanket, closed the hut door, and set off to Qualla. Both Dawn and Daniel were not happy at taking the girl with us, telling me there was more than one snake at that house.

After about half an hour, the five of us reached a large sign that told us we were entering the reservation, which was in the valley just beyond the sign. We stood looking into the valley, where we could see a group of buildings forming a village. Some of the buildings were round in shape, quite large with thatched roofs. Others were smaller wooden houses with zinc rooftops. Dawn called me over to look at the sign and started reading the information below the name of the Qualla Reservation. I could hear a note of sadness in her voice as she read about the displacement of her people.

"The Cherokee domain once extended beyond the distant mountains, but the white man, with broken treaties and fruitless promises, brought trouble to the Indians and caused their banishment to an Oklahoma reservation. A few escaped capture and fled into the Great Smokies, eventually forming the Eastern Band that now live in the valley below."

After edging our way down the steep slope, we reached the village. A lot of children came running up to us, excited by the visiting strangers. There was a large fire in the centre of the village and everyone was going about their daily business. It was like taking a step back in time to see an authentic Indian settlement. Two men came forward to find out who we were and after Dawn and Daniel spoke with them for a few moments, we were led to a large, thatched circular house in the middle of the widespread village. Dawn explained we were being taken to the chief, whose name was Black Wolf. A tall, muscular man in his early forties came out and welcomed us. He said, "I will draw thorns from your feet. We will walk the white path of life together. Like a brother of my own blood, I will love you. I will wipe tears from your eyes when you are sad. I will put your aching heart to rest."

Dawn told us this was an old Cherokee prayer to greet travellers. We thanked him and after holding our hands and hugging us, invited us into his house. We all sat on a handwoven rug in the centre of the floor.

Black Wolf looked me straight in the eyes and asked, "Chiane, my child, have you brought the words of the ancient ones?"

I answered "yes" and quickly took the pouch containing the crystal out of my backpack and handed it to the chief. I thought he would open it straight away, but he placed it, still in the pouch, on a stone, which was surrounded by various herbs and leaves, covering it with a red cloth. He then proceeded to light a fire in a vessel next to the stone while chanting a few Cherokee wordsI could not understand, before sitting back down with us on the rug. He called for food and drink and offered it to us, which Dawn told us we must partake in, as it would be an insult not to. We broke bread together and ate it along with a selection of meats and some herbal tea. Daniel told the chief about the old man in the hut, and Black Wolf quickly despatched some men to fetch him, telling them to arrange a funeral pyre. He gave the girl a deerskin pouch, similar to the medicine bags Dawn had given us, and told the girl her father was at rest with the spirits. The girl nodded and thanked the chief. I noticed she had never left Dusty's side ever since leaving the hut in the mountains, and sat clinging onto his arm.

Through Crystal Clear Waters

Black Wolf told us about his great-great-grandfather, Tsali, and how he had led his people into the mountains. He told us that he, just like his grandfather, was a warrior chief and would do anything, even give up his life, for his people. He then went on to tell us that tomorrow, after the funeral of the old man; we would celebrate the words of the ancient ones. We would drum, dance, and hold a powwow. Daniel informed us we would be beside the chief at this ceremony as guests of honour and would partake in the peace pipe.

A place to sleep was prepared for us; several women came to escort us to where we would spend the night. I was in one house with Dawn, and Dusty was sharing the house next to ours with Daniel. The girl refused to leave Dusty's side, so eventually, after much discussion, was allowed to stay in his house. I could see that Dusty had taken quite a shine to this young woman, but Dawn and Daniel didn't seem to like her at all. We all settled down, waiting for what tomorrow may bring.

Chapter 23

Enlightenment

When morning broke, there was a lot of hustle and bustle going on in the village. I stepped outside the door to see a lovely sunny day. A large funeral pyre had been built on the outskirts of the community, and I could see the form of the old man wrapped in a colourful cloth lying on the top.

I went across to one of the large square houses, where there were a lot of people outside. It was a communal house where people would meet and have refreshment. I got a coffee and went outside to smoke a cigarette. Dusty was already outside, with the girl still clinging on to him like a shadow. I wondered if she had left him alone while sleeping, but I put that thought straight out my mind, as the pictures it conjured up were embarrassing. Anyway, she had just lost her father and so was bound to cling to someone.

I went over to sit with them, asking Dusty if he had found out her name yet. He said she had not spoken, apart from saying "thank you" when he gave her a drink. Dawn and Daniel came over, telling us the funeral would take place in an hour and that after that had been done, we would be getting ready for the celebration of the crystal message in the afternoon with Chief Black Wolf.

After a while, we all went to sit in the circle around the funeral pyre. Every member of the tribe was gathered, including all the chiefs and elders who sat opposite us. One of the elders lit the fire under the pyre, and a lot of drumming and chanting took place while the flames consumed the old man. All this went on for about forty-five minutes.

Afterward, we went to sit on the veranda of the communal house for another cigarette. Dusty was asking if he could get a beer from anywhere. Daniel told him alcohol was not allowed, but we would get plenty to eat and drink at the celebration. Suddenly, the girl stood up and faced Dusty, looking at him directly, and said, "Marla." He looked puzzled, so she repeated, "Marla that is my name."

Dusty held out his hand, saying, "Oh, pleased to meet you, Marla." She shook his hand, smiled, and promptly sat back down next to him. I had thought it strange she had not shown any emotion at her father's funeral, and was now smiling at Dusty as if she had just met him for the first time. Daniel told us

Enlightenment

we must go prepare for the ceremony and so to follow him to the medicine man to be cleansed. We got up, walking with him to a big round house on the edge of the village, Marla tried to follow, but Daniel told her to stay back in a very stern way, which seemed to result in her sulking. We entered the large house, I thought we might be having a shower, but I was wrong.

On entering, we were greeted by an old man in his seventies. In the centre of the house was a fire, set in a circle of stones. There were numerous pots and jars containing herbs, bones, and all sorts of stuff, the smoke rising out of a central hole in the top of the house. There were animal skulls hanging from the thatched roof and a lot of brightly coloured rugs on the walls. We were told by the medicine man to sit on a rug near the fire and were given a large bowl to place on the floor in front of us. Dusty and I looked at each other. We did not know what to expect, and the whole atmosphere was very foreboding. The medicine man then gave us each a vessel containing some sort of liquid and told us to drink. The stuff smelt awful, but not wanting to offend, we put the vessel to our lips and took a sip. The medicine man was waving his hands in a motion to tell us we must drink it all. It tasted disgusting, and glancing at Dusty, I could tell by the expression on his face he did not like it, either. Dusty nodded at me, so we both took a deep breath and swallowed the rest of the liquid. Within moments, I realised what the bowls were for, as we were both violently sick. This seemed to please the medicine man, as he was smiling and clapping. When we were done vomiting, we were given a drink of water and a cloth, and I was just pleased the ordeal was over. The old man told us we were now cleansed and so could take part in the ceremony. We thanked him, although I didn't know why thanks were needed for making us vomit. We left the house.

Outside, I said to Dusty, "They could have warned us that were going to happen."

"I know," he replied. "I wasn't expecting that. Who knows what's going to happen at this ceremony?" I thought, surely nothing horrible could occur at a joyous event. I would have to wait and see. Marla ran up to us and quickly started wiping Dusty's face with a cloth in a very caring way.

Dawn came up to me to say she was going to get me ready and told Dusty to go with Daniel to prepare. I was beginning to worry what I now would be expected to do, but she seemed to pick up on my caution and told me, "Don't worry; you are just going to get showered and dressed."

I breathed a sigh of relief as we went into the house in which I had spent last night. I looked across at Dusty

Enlightenment

as he was entering his house with Daniel, Marla was not allowed in, so sat down in a grumpy mood on the steps outside the door, and I had to smile.

Inside, I was told to strip off and get into a homemade shower cubical, which was just a wooden frame covered with deerskin. Inside the cubical was a small zinc bath. I looked up to see a pipe pointing down at me. Dawn shouted, "Are you ready?"

I told her I was, so she started pumping a handle that sent water down through the pipe. It was quite cold, but also refreshing after the vomiting process and much appreciated. Dawn said the water came from a mountain spring and was said to have healing properties. This put me in mind of the spa I had visited while in Jamaica.

When the shower was finished, she gave me a towel to dry myself off and laid out some clothes on the bed for me to wear. There was a long red embroidered skirt, a beige blouse with beads sewn all over it, and some beige moccasins. After I dressed, Dawn began to braid my hair with beads and brightly coloured cords, which had feathers attached to the ends. After she had completed my hair, she said, "There, all finished."

I asked if there was a mirror. She fetched one from inside a large cupboard. I looked at myself, thinking

Through Crystal Clear Waters

I resembled an Indian woman from one of the old Western movies I had seen. But I was impressed, wishing I had my camera with me so I could show the children when I returned home. They would never believe their mother looked like an Indian squaw! Dawn told me to rest now while she got ready, then she would come back and escort me to the ceremony. She told me I could have a cigarette on the front step, but not to eat anything before we were to gather. Then off she went.

I went outside to light up on the steps and saw Dusty already outside his house, smoking. He looked splendid in a beige tunic and trousers, decorated with deerskin fringes and brightly coloured motifs. He, too, was wearing moccasins, and his shoulder-length hair was tied back with a long braid with feathers hanging from it. He had a red headband round his forehead. He stood up, holding his hands out, smiling, so I could take a good look at him. I, too, stood up and twirled around to show him, and he clapped his hands.

Soon Dawn and Daniel came back, both splendidly dressed, similar to myself and Dusty, but they both wore full traditional Indian headdresses made from many eagle feathers, which flowed down their backs to their waists. Dawn told me these were to signify their rank of chief to their tribe. Daniel also had face paint on, which symbolised a warrior.

We were escorted to the ceremony, where the whole of the Eastern Band sat in a circle around a huge bonfire. While the majority were seated on the ground, Chief Black Wolf sat on a chair with a large spear at his side. There were four more chairs, two on each side of the chief. Dawn and Daniel sat on his right-hand side. Dusty and I were invited to sit in the chairs on his left-hand side. Behind Black Wolf was a bench with six men who looked like very important tribal elders. This whole setup told me that Dusty and I were guests of honour at this ceremony, which made me feel both proud and excited.

The whole crowd sat in utter silence until Chief Black Wolf stood up to address the congregation. "My family," he began. "I ask you to welcome the Crystal Child Chiane and the Star Child Dusty." He turned, taking both our hands, bringing us forward to stand on either side of him, raising our hands above our heads. The whole crowd started clapping and whooping.

After everyone calmed down, the chief led us back to our seats and continued. "As our ancestors prophesied, the Crystal Child will deliver to us the words of wisdom from the ancient ones and will be guided and protected by the Star Child. That time has come to pass. Last night, I received the words from these descendants of our past, Chiane and Dusty. They have overcome many dangerous obstacles to fulfil this prophesy, and I ask you all to give them their due respect while they spend time with us." Everyone again clapped and cheered, and I could feel myself blushing. Black Wolf then went on. "My family, from the beginning of time, we have been preparing for this day—protecting our beliefs, enduring great hardships, and since my great-grandfather, Tsali, took his people to these mountains to be keepers of the prophesy, having to hide like cowards to prevent our heritage from being destroyed forever. Now is the time for our work to begin, as the dawning of the Age of Awareness is here. Soon will come the time when all the people of the world will become aware of the Great Spirit and will attempt to seek the truth.

"Our job is to enable this process, and I will instruct you and guide your footsteps over the coming weeks. We have fourteen moons to do this preparation work, before the great day when we will gather to unite with the sacred wisdoms, which are carved from crystal formed in the shape of men's skulls. On that day, humanity will begin the journey it is destined to take; we shall be reunited with the ancient ones. The world will begin its new cycle and evil will be outcast."

Enlightenment

Everyone stood up cheering and clapping. Dusty and I looked at each other. It was obvious we were had same thought. This was about what we had done by finding the crystal and delivering it to its rightful keeper, Black Wolf. These people saw us to be of great importance. The chief had said we were Crystal and Star Children. This all seemed so unreal, and I wondered if I was dreaming. I pinched myself.

Dusty whispered to me, "I've got a feeling this is just the beginning."

I had to agree. The crystal I had delivered to the chief was not a skull; it was a pyramid. The chief had spoken of the dawning of awareness and work to be done. Was our part in this over? From the way Black Wolf spoke, I doubted it. In fourteen months it would be December 2012, the time of the prophesy of the Mayans, the Age of Aquarius and the Awakening. Dusty took my hand and smiled, telling me we would see this through together. I felt a sense of calm.

The chief then took his spear decorated with eagle feathers, thrusting it into the ground in front of him, and the celebrations began. A group of four women began beating a large drum, while twelve young men, all wearing face paint, danced around the fire. People began singing and chanting. Food and drink were brought to everyone around the chief, and what a spread it was. There was wild boar, chicken and beef, roasted sweet potatoes, and plenty of fruits and vegetables. There were also jugs of a type of mead, which was made with honey but not fermented, and seemed to please Dusty as we all tucked in.

In the evening, nearly all of the middle-aged women did the Stomp Dance. All in multi-coloured attire, they slowly moved around the fire in an anticlockwise direction, while others beat the drum and sang a song. This was truly a spectacular sight and sent shivers down my back. I was very moved. Later, both Dusty and I were invited to join in the dancing with many of the tribe, who all wanted to hold our hands as a note of respect. A great bald eagle was spotted circling above us, which excited everyone, believing it to be a sign from the Great Spirit. I had noticed, throughout this activity that Marla had a face like thunder, and had not realy joned in with any of it, but just put this down to the fact she was not allowed to accompany Dusty.

A little time after the eagle sighting, a familiar face joined us, warmly welcomed by the chief. It was Isaac. He was familiarly dressed in a white toga with a golden waist braid and sandals which crisscrossed up his calves, just as I had seen in my dream of the gathering. He turned to Dusty and I, telling us we had done well and that he would speak to us

Enlightenment

tomorrow, as now he had work to do. After grabbing a chicken leg and cup of mead, Isaac went with Black Wolf and the elders that were sat on the bench, taking their leave to enter the chief's house. Dawn told us they were going for a council meeting. She invited Dusty and me to accompany her, and Daniel to join the remaining chiefs for a powwow. We accepted, and while everyone else continued dancing and feasting, we went with all the chiefs to another circular house, not far from the medicine man's house.

Once inside, everyone sat on rugs, again in a circle. A couple of the chiefs began packing large pipes with some sort of ground leaf. They lit them and started smoking. After taking a few draws, they began passing this peace pipe round the circle. When it came to our turn, Daniel told us, "Smoke. You have earned the right. It will enlighten your minds to your purpose and destiny."

So we both partook. It had a very pleasant taste, and I immediately began to feel euphoric. By the time the pipe came round for the third time I was quite "high" and noticed some of the chiefs had laid back on their blankets. I turned to speak to Dusty, but he too had lay back with a contented expression on his face. I would be the only one awake if this went on, I thought. Dawn took another draw of the pipe, then passed it to me, saying, "All will be revealed tomorrow after the crystal council, but for now, enlighten yourself."

I took one more draw and felt myself relaxing back into my blanket. I could not move. I began to try and concentrate to stop myself falling into this weird sensation, but I could not control it. My mind was buzzing; I was in a rainbow haze and felt myself being drawn to a bright blue light. From it, there were portholes to look out on various aspects of life. One by one, I peered into these portholes; I actually saw life on Atlantis, the legendary continent. It was if I was some sort of god looking down. I saw Izacal as a child being taught by his father. I saw the greedy and power- hungry downfall, and the twelve Star Keepers and Planet Trackers fleeing at night in their boats to twelve different directions. I saw Atlantis destroyed by a massive volcano on an island nearby, forcing a landmass into the sea and causing a great tsunami that engulfed the whole continent, forcing it to the bottom of the ocean with all lives lost.

Now, I seemed to be travelling through a time tunnel, every now and again stopping to view yet another event in human history. I encountered the horrific effects of many wars, oppression, and slavery. I saw poverty matched against opulence, decisions made that led millions to fight for causes they did not

Enlightenment

understand. I saw how we are all manipulated by our leaders and indoctrinated from birth in their beliefs. How all previous civilisations, after reaching their height, succumbed to the same downfall.

I saw all the harms that were inflicted on the people of the world. But I also saw all the good that had been done, proving there was hope for humanity. I became aware of the power of the masses—how when the "little people" of the world awake to the lies and the indoctrinations, they would realise their own power and rise up against those who oppress them. These little people would demand to be heard. They would select who led them, and all the evil would be cast out.

I was shown two scenes. The first was a rich garden, with trees, flowers, and rolling green hills. Everyone was happy, war was a thing of the past, and every soul was equal. The second scene was of war and disaster; people lived in poverty and misery. They were at the mercy of evil dictators who would kill them if they tried to fight back. As I stood looking at these two scenes, I could see a signpost in between. Two pointers indicated opposite directions—one toward the paradise garden, one toward the hell of war and disaster. At first, I could not discern any writing on them. I strained my mind to get closer and saw a single word appear—*choose.*

Feeling myself moving forward, I knew instinctively that these paths were mankind's options. I had the knowledge of everything, past and present. Now, I was entering a white light and could perceive many people—some with physical form, others just like energy, but I could still identify with them. The knowledge of the universe was laid out before me, and I understood. I knew at that instant who I was, why I was here, and what I must do.

I was a Crystal Child. I saw my genetic mother and father and all the generations before them—some in physical form, some pure energy, and had a vision of Izacal placing me in a cot at the hospital as a baby. I also saw Dusty's ancient history, how he was destined to protect me and accompany me on many journeys. He too was special. He was a Star Child.

Dusty was from the family of Star Keepers, and I of the Planet Trackers. Our work was not yet done. It was just beginning. When Black Wolf revealed the wisdom of the ancients tomorrow, after scrying the crystal, we would know what our ultimate destiny would be, and also the destiny of earth and humanity.

Chapter 24

Into the Future

I abruptly roused from the visions, sat up, and looked around me. All the chiefs were still lying on their rugs, apparently sleeping, but there was no sign of Dusty. I tiptoed out of the house to find him. After a few minutes, I spotted him on the steps of the communal house, gazing at the sky, smoking a cigarette, and eating a piece of cake. I went and sat down next to him, asking him if he was okay. He offered me a cigarette, telling me he felt a bit strange and that he now understood what it must be like for me, as he'd had the weirdest dream. It hadn't even felt like a dream. He believed it to be the result of the peace pipe. I asked him what he had seen in his dream, believing he'd had the same one as me. But although some parts were similar, such as mankinds past wars and the destruction of civilisations, there were other bits that were totally different.

He told me about the introduction of the Gregorian calendar, which had caused disharmony for the people of the world. Pope Gregory XIII had changed the calendar, taking out ten days to align the Easter festival with the spring equinox. But, as Dusty had learned, the reasons went a bit deeper than that. It had been the result of an earlier doctrine of the church, declaring that all non-Christians were sub-standard humans and enemies of Christianity. This had been the mindset of Christian nations when they conquered many native lands, killing, raping, and pillaging, and destroying beliefs, languages, and ultimately the understanding of nature.

The church took dominance, deeming themselves to be saviours of tribes around the world. They forced Christianity onto those communities in an attempt to make them comply. They enacted many atrocities on native peoples, including slavery, though the church appeared to speak out against them, hiding the fact they were to blame. The reform of the calendar was the next step to unbalance nature, making it easier to manipulate.

The church added more months to the calendar, which threw the seasons out of sync, thus forcing the people to turn to leaders for guidance. But the leaders of empires were also engaged in this disharmony and oppression.

Into the Future

Man now had control of time. Native peoples had used the readings of the stars and the nature of Earth to know when to plant and harvest, or when to expect droughts or flooding. But with the imposition of the change of time, it created havoc—not just to the seasons, but to man himself. Humans had a natural body clock, affected by the moon and the tides. Women had a menstrual cycle and the cycle of pregnancy, taking nine moons from conception to birth. And life had a cycle from cradle to grave. Plants, animals, humans, and even Earth itself had these cycles.

But a few men played God, manipulating the calendar to control the masses, and over the years, the whole world adapted to the twelve-month, sixty-minute concept of time, governed by the banks and the stock exchanges. The whole monetary system relied on this manmade concept of time. Our leaders were even abusing their own systems out of greed. And the people have been manipulated over generations to accept this disorder.

But just like everything else, the age of Christian imperialism was about to conclude its cycle. Not the belief in God or the Great Spirit—this was Alpha and Omega, and had been since the beginning of the universe. But the age of manmade religion would come to an end. In 2012, at the winter solstice, the age of Pisces would give way to a new cycle, the Age of Aquarius—the age of humanity. The people of the world would wake up from all the years of lies and indoctrination and realise the truth that had been hidden from them. They would see the plans of the evil, power- hungry few. They would realise the plan for "One World, One Law, One Rule" and that their part in this ultimate plan would be little more than as puppets that dance for the elite few.

These days, time meant money—not for the masses, but for the few. The whole economic system was based around this twelve-month, sixty-minute system. But the whole setup was about to collapse, especially when the people of the world wake up and rebel against it.

I listened as Dusty told me of all his visions, and when he had finished I said, "Oh my God. I can see how all this fits in."

He turned and looked me straight in the eye, seeming very concerned. "Chi, this is terrible. I have heard of the world globalisation conspiracy theory, where the elite few rule and control the whole world. But this information fills in the gaps and puts credence to it. It's a bit like finding the lost pieces of a jigsaw puzzle."

We both sat in silence, trying to digest all we had seen. Everywhere was quiet, everyone asleep. Only

Into the Future

Dusty and I were left here alone with our thoughts. We both looked up at the night sky, gazing at the constellations, wishing we could work out the answers in the stars, just like the Mayans had when constructing their calendars. We wondered what the crystal would tell us later in the day.

After a while, Dusty said the whole experience had worn him out, saying he had the munchies. There was some great chocolate cake in the communal house, and he asked me if I wanted some. I had to admit that I felt hungry too, so we got some coffee and cake, and as neither of us felt like sleeping, took it onto the veranda, deciding to watch the sun rise.

The village slowly woke up and went about its day. Dawn and Daniel joined us later in the morning, all of us waiting for Black Wolf to summon us to his house. The waiting seemed to go on forever and I felt quite impatient. Then, at around three in the afternoon, Isaac came to speak with us. He said they had been working on the crystal all night and would soon be ready to share some of that information with us.

"Some?" I asked him.

"You will be given all you need to know," he replied. "Some of the information will be irrelevant to you, but right now I need something to eat."

I laughed and asked him if he had been smoking peace pipes. He said they had not been smoking, only drinking tea, and that he had not eaten the last couple of days, apart from the chicken leg when he got here. Dusty told him he should try the chocolate cake, and we all went into the communal house. Marla attempted to join us, but Isaac told her she was not allowed. She went off in a huff, much to the relief of Dusty, who was tucking into yet another piece of chocolate cake.

We had to wait another two hours before Black Wolf was ready. I must have been moaning about how long it was taking, since Dusty told me to remember what he had said last night about time, and to quit complaining. Good things were worth waiting for. Finally, Isaac, Dusty, and I were summoned to the chief's house. We all sat gathered around the crystal with a few of the elders.

Black Wolf told us that a good proportion of the information related to the first three cycles, beginning from the year 3114 BC. Another part was about agriculture, in the early part of the fourth cycle. He didn't think any of that information was of any use to us. But he said he would reveal the present and future information, asking if we were ready to hear it. We confirmed we were more than ready and settled in, eager to hear what he had to say.

Into the Future

The first thing he told us was the need to ignore all the media hype about the supposed Mayan apocalypse prophesied for the year 2012. For a start, all the Mayans had predicted for the end of the fourth cycle was the planetary alignment at the winter solstice, when the sun, Earth, and Venus would come together at the centre of the Milky Way, marking the start of a fifth cycle. They had also made reference to dramatic weather changes and astronomical events such as solar flares, and changes to the Earth's poles and magnetism. But they had never given any dates or timelines or ever said these things would come all at once and destroy the Earth.

"In fact," he said, "the most important thing they had said about events leading up to the winter solstice 2012 was that people would start to question their place in the order of things."

"Like what?" I asked.

"We will see protests and riots in countries we would least expect to see them, in places that have strong dictators, like the Middle East or the former Soviet Union, and also in the opulent Western world," he continued. "There will be a breakdown of the whole world's monetary systems, which will cause even more riots, as those who are responsible for errors made will try to put the responsibility onto the shoulders of the working classes and the poor, elderly, or sick. The rich will not want to give up their wealth, and this will create splits in government. In the West, leaders will try to rectify their mistakes by withdrawing money for health, education, welfare, and policing. This, in turn, will lead to more crime, and people feeling unsafe. The governments will declare civil unrest and bring the Army onto the streets to maintain order. This will leave the door open to foreign attack from an unexpected enemy."

The chief went on. "A large continent will rise up. These are the ones who hold the purse strings and own most of the debts incurred by certain counties. During the first part of the new cycle, we will see riots, civil war, crime, drugs, and general unrest around the world. But these things must come to pass for the new cycle to move forward. Humanity has to wake up. A new cycle means a new order and a new way of life. The winter solstice and the fifth cycle is the start of humanity demanding their rights. It is a time of great change. The age of humanity will not happen overnight—it will take many years to have enough impact to make the needed changes. But it *will* happen. The people of the old worlds will be consulted on the way forward, and it is they who will begin the awakening," Black Wolf explained.

Into the Future

"We will have to endure much more disaster, encountering tsunamis, earthquakes, and extreme weather. Where there was once fertile land, there will be drought. Where there were once deserts, nature will start to spring, and where there was once ice, there will be green pastures. These things must come to pass, as it is the nature of the universe, but it is *not* the end of the Earth. The magnetic field of the Earth will be edging to a new direction. This will be a slow process, in order to enable humans to adjust. But it will slow down communication and the exchange of money around the world.

"We will see many new diseases; some caused by climate changes, others by man's corruption of nature, both accidentally and intentionally. People will turn their backs on their religions; they will not turn from their belief in God or the Great Spirit, but from the lies of men who pretend to deliver the words of God. People will turn their backs on education, preferring to teach their own offspring to protect them from indoctrination. They will turn their backs on modern medicine, not trusting their health services and turning instead to more natural sources. They will also turn their backs on communication devices, realising they are a way of watching, manipulating, and controlling the masses. People will seek the truth," the chief stressed.

He went on. "This has already begun, and will continue to do so for many years, as the future of humanity is in the hands of Earth's children not yet born. But we must plant the seeds for the future generations; we must awaken for the new cycle. The people of today and tomorrow will plant the seeds, helped by Mother Nature and the ancients, helped by the Crystals and the Star Children, and helped by God and the Great Spirit. By the end of the fifth cycle, humanity will be back in tune with the nature of the universe and enter the utopia.

"Yes, the fifth cycle does bring an apocalypse, but in the true meaning of the word. We have been taught that the word means death and destruction, and it causes fear. But the true meaning of *apocalypse* is *that which is already there but has been hidden*. The apocalypse is *truth.*

Dusty stated he had read the true definition of the word apocalypse, and that was indeed what it meant, and that things were beginning to make sense to him now. I myself had always thought that it had meant total anialation, but knowing my friend was a walking encyclopedia, realised that this was the real meaning. I questioned why it was we were all lead to believe the doom and disaster version, to which Dusty answered, "Keep up Chi, we have been conditioned by fear, it is a way of relying on those in power." I had to smile to myself as it seemed Dusty was coming round to what he always said was my crazy way of thinking, or was it that my thoughts were not as weird as they had appeared to be.

"The Age of Aquarius," the chief explained, "will last until the year forty-one-seventy-two. The actual date of the fruition of the age of awareness is in the year twenty-one-fifty. This was calculated using linear versus synchronic time, and following the natural laws of the universe. The crystal speaks of the sixth cycle, but without definite clarity. The future of the sixth depends on the outcome of the fifth. It shows two paths—one good, the other bad. There is a third path which will be the consequences of decisions made by people in the fifth cycle. The Crystal Children have seen the visions of the two paths. If the right decisions are made, the future will be peaceful and harmonic, evil will be eradicated, and there will be no more oppression, poverty, or crime. A new world, where everyone will be equal and feel contented."

Next, Black Wolf explained, we were to learn of an event due to take place to enable this transformation. He sent the other elders away, leaving just Dusty, Isaac, and me. He poured us some tea, telling us it would help us visualise the more intricate details of what we were going to hear and help us understand our roles. But first we must wait for a visitor who was going to relay this information and guide us.

The tea tasted strange—quite strong in flavour, but palatable. I asked the chief what kind of tea leaves they were. He told me they were the same leaves as were in the peace pipe. They were coca leaves and had been used by the Mayan elders to communicate with the ancients. They were harmless and in no way in the same category as cocaine available on the streets today, which was a corrupted version of the drug.

We drank the tea. It did not make us feel high but gave us a rejuvenating and relaxing effect. We sat waiting for this mysterious guest, with the chief offering more tea, which we duly accepted.

By the time we were on our third cup, a man in a hooded cloak entered. Isaac got to his feet, giving the man a warm hug. After the man greeted the chief, he turned to me, dropping his hood so I could see his face. I was too shocked for words, as the man who stood before me smiling was Izacal.

"But…you are real," I stammered.

He laughed and replied, "I am what I wish to be at any given time. Now are you going to introduce me to your friend?"

I turned to Dusty. "This is Izacal, my spirit guide."

Into the Future

I thought Dusty would think I was imagining things and start laughing, but he got up and hugged Izacal, welcoming him. Once everyone was again seated and I had got over the shock of seeing the person of my dreams in the flesh, Izacal began to explain.

He told us that Dusty and I were part of his family—that we were both descendants of the Star Keepers and Planet Trackers from the thirteen planets, working for millions of years to harmonise the universe. There were many descendants here on Earth; all waiting for the time humans would be ready to understand the universal laws. Dusty was a Star Child, born to human parents, but had a gene that lay dormant, only to be awakened at the right time, when he made a connection with his counterpart. His duty was to protect, enable, and help this counterpart to fulfil his or her duties. His counterpart was a Crystal Child.

I was that Crystal Child, born with no parental or genetic background, with pure ancient genes. The Crystal Children were the ones who preached peace and those designated to protect and look after the vessels of knowledge—the crystals. Together we were both Star Children, and there were many on Earth. Some would never awaken but would continue procreating the genes. Others would never accept who they were or had become corrupted. Some of the Star Children were already active, and had been so since the 1960s. The Crystal Children were not so many in numbers and took a long time to realise their destiny, although all through their growing, they knew they were different. All Crystal Children had dreams that enabled them to communicate with the ancients.

The children of the Earth, Izacal explained, were in their adolescence, the preparation for the fifth cycle that was to begin on the winter solstice of 2012. He said it was the duty of all active Star Children to guide the adolescent Earth children into their coming-of-age, so they can the lead the life of harmony and peace that the universe intended.

People of Earth, Izacal added, believed they were the only planet with intelligent life, but were not. But towards the end of time, billions of years away, they would be. Earthlings were the youngest and would be the last. The Star Children must make sure the fifth transition took place, or Earth would be doomed to misery and destruction.

Of the thirteen planets, only seven survived, Izacal told us, some with only spirit-like populations. What happened to the other six should be held as a lesson of what not to do. Four of the long-gone planets had taken the path of war and greed, causing misery and wiping out all of their civilisations. One of those planets had become so obsessed with technology, creating weapons of mass destruction and causing its own end in a massive nuclear explosion, which reduced it to wandering rocks that would eternally float round the universe. The last planet, where life was now extinct, had been called Hellibu. The people who lived there, the Hellibuans, had been similar in stature to humans, but were reptilian, having scales instead of skin. The Hellibuans became so obsessed with power that they tried to eradicate any of the populace they deemed to be substandard. They created diseases to wipe out certain sectors of their planet and over time were so successful that they eradicated all but about one hundred of their species. This left them with no one to oppress, rule, or control, so they started fighting among themselves until their number reduced to six. Those had been the cleverest of all Hellibuans, and with nothing left on their own planet, they went in search of a new world. What better than young planet Earth? It was a place where they could mould and control a population that was just beginning their evolution. The same six Hellibuans were on Earth today. They never aged and, unless killed, would live forever. They were pure evil and had taken on human form. They would lead Earth's children into misery and destruction. Although they had learnt from their past mistakes, their intent was to prevent Earth's children from awakening, so they could manipulate them to a point where the whole of humanity would be nothing more than their slaves. At that time they would rename Earth in honour of their old planet, Izacal warned us. They would call it *hell.*

The Star Children had to destroy these Hellibuans, or at least make humanity aware by exposing them. It would be the task of the Crystal Children to determine who they were, as they remained hidden. But all Star Children, he said, had to remain vigilant, as Hellibuans hated Star Children and would kill them. We would find them by their wealth, as they held the greatest percentage of the world's assets. They were surrounded by armies of wealthy humans who did their bidding, believing they themselves held power. But they too hid behind frontmen who were nothing but fall guys for the evil ones. At times, these people, whom the masses thought were leading them or had voted for to be in charge and responsible, were nothing more than puppets, controlled by the humans that answer to the Hellibuans.

Izacal told Dusty and I that we were the fifth awakened Star Children, and that there were another four pairs of Star and Crystal Children we must unite with. We would enable humanity to awaken and start the revolution in the human mind, destroy all evil, and enter the new age of peace and harmony.

"And there is one more thing," Izacal added.

Into the Future

There was a final crystal to find. This one held the instructions for the Grand Gathering I had seen in my dream, when all the universal crystals came together in the shape of human skulls and would reveal the future of Mother Earth to representatives from around the globe, and to ancients and spirits. The final crystal pyramid was located somewhere in India, and we were to join the other Star Children to find it and deliver it to its keeper in Tibet, at the base of the Himalayas.

I looked at Izacal, telling him everything was now fitting into place, and asking him if was he, who left me at the hospital as a baby. He answered, "Yes, you are of pure blood and of my own family of Planet Trackers."

After questioning why I had not been made aware of this earlier in life, he explained everything had a time, and if I had not been busy with my earthly life, maybe that time would have been sooner, but the quest I had just undertaken would not have happened before this time, also destiny I am about to fulfil with Dusty, could not have been undertaken any earlier.

He then told both me and Dusty, we need to go and make plans for our next journey. Both Dawn and Daniel were going to spend some time in the Qualla with Black Wolf, and Isaac was going to take us back to Dusty's home, we would have just two months to make preparations for our next quest in India. We bid goodbye to Izacal and went outside.

Marla was stood waiting for Dusty, and I asked him what he was going to do about her. He said she should stay with her own people and went over to talk to her. I watched as he told her he was leaving, I expected her to be upset, but she got very angry, taking out a knife, which she tried to thrust into Dusty's back as he walked away. I screamed at him as she raised the knife, he instantly threw himself to the ground, rolling out of her way. Daniel came running across, pushed her to the ground, taking the knife out of her hand. I helped Dusty to his feet, and when we all turned to ask Marla what that was all about, she wasn't there. Instead, on the ground was a large green lizard, which quickly ran into the bush. Daniel explained, he had caught her going through Dusty's bag on the first night, he had never trusted her and had mentioned it to the medicine man, who told him he had known the old man that had died, and he did not have a daughter. Daniel believed she was an evil spirit sent to prevent us from delivering the crystal. By this time Black Wolf and Izacal joined us. The chief took both mine and Dusty's hand saying, "I fear this is only the first battle we will have to fight before this is over."

With a final farewell, we set off with Isaac back to Dusty's home.

Chapter 25

The Star Children

The journey back to Dusty's passed quickly as we chatted to Isaac about the time spent with the Cherokee. I learnt that the warning I had been given by Mytrle on my flight to Jamaica, was to enlighten me about both Ben and Marla, and was told to be aware of that in the future.

I asked Isaac how he knew of my conversation with Myrtle; he just smiled and replied, "She is one of us, as is Kendrick, who you will meet up with later in your quest." He went on, "there is no time to waste, you have just two months before you fly to India, and from that time you will only have twelve months to find the final crystal and get it to its keeper." He assured both me and Dusty, he would be with us from time to time, and Izacal would instruct me as to what to do. Also we would not be alone on this one, as other Star Children would meet us and we would all play a part in this final piece of information.

Through Crystal Clear Waters

Although the task ahead seemed daunting, it did not faze me, as for the first time in my life, I felt like I 'fitted in'. I had a purpose and was inspired to see it through. I glanced at Dusty; he smiled and gave me a hug. I was glad that we were to do this together, it was his job to protect me, and I always trusted him to do that.

After Isaac had dropped us off, I rang my children to tell them I would be returning in a few days. They were relieved at this information, but I thought it better to tell them in person I would be setting off again, this time to Asia.

The next couple of days, Dusty set up a joint account with the money Ben had been paid by the cartels, saying it would provide us with what we needed on our travels. He booked a flight for both of us to England, as he didn't believe we should be separated from now on, and it will help with my telling the kids I was going again, reminding me that this next trip we would be gone for at least one year.

Dusty tied up things his end and when everything was finalised we flew back to England, spending a good few weeks with the children, who were not too happy about us going on another 'Dig' but eventually got used to the idea. We all had a great time together, going out for meals and taking the grandchildren out on adventures. The children always had a soft spot for 'Uncle Dusty', and had considered him part of the family. But we kept our revelation of being Star Children and our destiny a secret, as we thought it something they would not understand.

When Dusty and I were alone, we mused over our first meeting all those years ago, and the escapades we had been through together. Dusty told me he had always considered me as his 'soul' friend and our friendship was 'meant to be'

I said our meeting must have been planned from the beginning of time and I finally knew who I was. 2012 will not be the end of the world, it is just the beginning.

It wasn't long before we were once again thundering down the runway, not knowing what challenges we were about to go through on our quest to awaken humanity.

I looked at Dusty. We both smiled and said in harmony, "Here we go again."

Made in the USA
Charleston, SC
09 May 2012